CASTLE ON THE Hill

A *Scarlet Cove* SEASIDE COZY MYSTERY

Agatha Frost
& Evelyn Amber

For questions and comments about this book, please contact
pinktreepublishing@gmail.com

www.pinktreepublishing.com
www.agathafrost.com
www.evelynamber.com

Edited by Keri Lierman and Karen Sellers
Proofread by Eve Curwen

ISBN: 9781973138372
Imprint: Independently published

A
Scarlet Cove
SEASIDE COZY MYSTERY

Book Two

One

Liz Jones pulled the paint-splattered yellow wool scarf tighter around her neck, the autumn breeze whipping up around her. She hurried to catch up to her friend, Nancy Turtle, as she speed-walked ahead in the dark like an excited child.

"*Come on!*" Nancy cried over her shoulder, grinning from ear to ear. "We don't want to be the last ones there."

Liz nodded, the icy breeze licking at her face. She glanced back at the coastal town of Scarlet Cove, which was nothing more than a mass of twinkling lights in the distance. Turning back to the looming castle on the hill, she marched forward with renewed energy, partly spurred on by her curiosity of the night ahead, and partly because her beagle, Paddy, was yanking on her arm.

"You do this every year on the night before Halloween?" Liz called into the wind as she caught up to Nancy. "The whole town?"

"The *whole* town," Nancy affirmed, her short, quirky fringe bouncing against her forehead right above the thick-rimmed glasses, which framed her round face. "For as long as anyone can remember."

Liz had only been living in Scarlet Cove for a little over two months since retiring from her city detective job, but she had come to accept that '*for as long as anyone can remember*' was as good an explanation as any. In those two months she had grown fond of Nancy, who despite only being thirty-four to Liz's forty-two, had a childlike quality that she had always found grating in other people, but found endearing in Nancy.

"And you all believe you're going to see ghosts?" Liz asked sceptically, scratching at her bushy red hair, which was tied lazily in a messy bun. "In Scarlet Cove? *Real* ghosts?"

"*Of course!*" Nancy exclaimed, slapping Liz on the shoulder in the way Liz had grown accustomed to. "Because of the legend."

"*The legend*," Liz echoed with a knowing nod. "It's all I've been hearing about in my shop all week."

Liz had moved to Scarlet Cove in the height of summer when the skies had been cloudless and blue long into the evening; it was what had attracted her to the tiny fishing town in the first place. Now that summer had passed, and autumn had taken hold, she had fallen in love with the early evening sunsets and the orangey-red leaves on the trees. Being a painter who ran her own arts and crafts shop in the heart of the town, she loved being able to dip into the warmer toned paints when she took her easel out on lazy Sunday afternoons. Over the past week, however, the chatter in her shop had not revolved around art, but the legend of Scarlet Cove Castle. She had heard the tale so many times she could now recite it by heart, not that she believed it much.

"A wealthy nobleman bought the castle hundreds of years ago," Nancy began, casting her hand to the giant stone structure as they got closer. "He lived there with his wife, and they were as happy as a couple could be. Like Jack and me, although I hope we don't end up like those two did. According to the legend, they were trying to start a family, but the wife was struggling to conceive. She was convinced it was her husband's fault, and she grew to resent him for it, so she started having it off with one of the cooks, hoping she would fall pregnant. The nobleman's only love was his wife, but the wife's only love was for the baby she couldn't have, and yet longed for."

"And then the nobleman found out his wife was messing around with the cook and he chopped her head off, the cook's head off, and everyone else's heads until the walls and hill were soaked in blood," Liz said quickly, waving her free hand dismissively. "I know the rest. It's a good story, I'll give you that."

"It's *true!*" Nancy cried, a little giggle behind her defiance. "It's where the name Scarlet Cove comes from, and it's been called that for as long as anyone can remember. It had a different name before that day, apparently. There was so much blood from all of the beheadings, the water in the cove was stained scarlet for *weeks*."

Liz pursed her lips, not wanting to burst her friend's bubble. She did not want to inform her that it would probably take the blood of tens of thousands to run down the hill, not soak into the soil, cross the rocks and sand, and then stain the water.

"It's a good story," Liz repeated. "Very imaginative."

The steep slope levelled out, allowing Liz to catch her breath. She had passed the castle many times on her evening walks with Paddy, but she had never seen it like this before. Someone had gone to the trouble of up-lighting the entire decaying medieval structure with blood-red floodlights. After fifteen years in the Greater Manchester Police, little scared Liz, but just looking up at the castle on the night before Halloween made her gulp a little.

She paused to scratch behind Paddy's ears as Nancy ran towards her boyfriend, Jack, who was on the edge of a group of what Liz could only guess was two hundred people, if not more. Fires burned in old barrels, vendors sold food from trucks, men handed cartoonish severed head balloons to children. A small part of Liz was surprised at the effort the town had put into celebrating an ancient tale, but a big part of her had come to expect nothing less from Scarlet Cove.

"What do you think, boy?" Liz muttered to Paddy. "Do you believe the legend?"

"Of course he does, babe!" a familiar squeaky Essex accent announced from behind her. "You need to book yourself in for another trim. It's split end city up in that ginger nest of yours."

Liz turned to Polly Spragg, who was bundled up in a bright pink overcoat, her peroxide blonde beehive jutting out from her make-up heavy face and unnatural orange tan. She was the owner of the Crazy Waves hair salon and had been cutting Liz's hair since her arrival in town.

"I think you might be right, Polly," Liz said with a small chuckle as she stood up fully, her eyes drifting to the man on Polly's arm. "You must be Polly's boyfriend. I've heard a lot about you."

"You have?" the man asked with an air of

disinterest, one eye on Liz, another on the castle. "Dare I ask?"

"I talk about you all the time at the salon, babe!" Polly giggled, slapping the man playfully on the chest, barely able to raise a smile from his stiff and sour expression. "Nathan, this is Liz. She's the one who owns the new arts and crafts shop, remember? Well, it's not so new anymore, but you must have heard of her."

Nathan forced a half-smile and jerked his head into what might have been a nod, not fully giving away if he had heard of Liz or not. She narrowed her eyes on the disinterested man, sure she had seen him somewhere in the town, but unable to place her finger on where exactly.

After promising to book an appointment sometime in the coming week, Liz let the couple overtake so she could watch them walk towards the ritual. Her mental image of Nathan had been completely shattered from the one in Polly's stories. The hair stylist was such a fun and upbeat girl, Liz had expected her boyfriend to be cut from the same cloth, but he looked like he could have sucked the fun out of his own birthday party. She could not remember the last time she had seen two people more unsuited to each other. Wondering if she had caught him on a bad day, she tightened her hand around the lead and tagged along behind.

Chatter and laughter swallowed her up as she walked into the vast stone courtyard, the red walls of the castle looming around the townsfolk. Distant music drifted in from concealed crackly speakers, and the scent of barbecued sausages and burgers pricked her and Paddy's noses.

She pushed through the bundled-up crowd until she found Nancy, who was draped across Jack. They were sitting on what appeared to be a fallen stone column, with Jack's best friend and local farmer, Simon, on his other side. Simon smiled meekly at Liz, and she smiled back, her stomach performing a somersault, making her wonder if she was really forty-two and not fourteen.

"*Get a grip of yourself, woman*," she whispered under her breath, pushing forward a wider smile. "Good to see you both."

"You too," Jack said, slurping from the mouth of a beer can as he reached out to scratch Paddy's head. "Didn't think you'd be the ghost hunting type, Liz."

"Oh, you know me," Liz said with a shrug as she looked around the crowd, sure the gathering was more an excuse to eat and be merry than actual ghost hunting. "I'll try anything once."

Liz perched on the cold stone next to Simon. They smiled clumsily at each other, like teenagers would in the school corridors. She cleared her throat and looked out at the crowd, focussing her attention on a group of young children who appeared to be re-enacting the night of the beheadings with a large stick and tomato ketchup stolen from one of the food trucks.

"I'm glad the weather has held up," Simon said, his cheeks blushing as he glanced up at the clear inky sky. "Rained non-stop last year."

Liz parted her lips, unsure how to respond. It had been two months since her shop's grand opening, and two months since her almost-kiss with Simon. In that moment behind her shop, after sampling one of Simon's delicious cheese nibbles created in her honour, she had wanted nothing more than for him to kiss her. Nancy had interrupted them before their lips had a chance to meet. They had not spoken about it since, even if it was written across their faces every time they were brought together.

"Beer?" Jack asked, reaching across to offer Liz one of an ice-cold dripping four-pack. "It's Scarlet Cove Brew."

"No, thanks."

"Liz doesn't like beer all that much," Simon said, reaching behind him into a zip-up cooler filled with ice. "Which is why I brought this."

He handed her a soggy box of wine, the melting ice having dampened the cardboard.

"Boxed wine," she noted unsurely. "I didn't know they still made this."

Simon blushed and glanced down at his feet, looking like a scorned child. Liz sighed, rolling her eyes at her own stiffness. She was not a snob when it came to wine; she usually bought whatever was cheapest with the strongest alcohol content. They were both adults, but neither of them seemed to know how to act like it.

"Here." Jack reached out and grabbed the box from Liz. "It's really just a bag in a box."

He tore off the soggy cardboard with ease before

passing it back to her. She looked down at the chilled bag of white wine, feeling like a drink was just what she needed.

"In for a penny," she said, passing Paddy's lead to Simon so she could tease the valve over her mouth. Cool white wine dribbled against her tongue, some spilling over the edge and running down her chin into her scratchy scarf. "It's not half bad, actually."

She winked at Simon, prompting him to grin, which flashed his trademark dimples. Seeing those soft dips in his flushed cheeks had an effect on her that she had spent the best part of the last two months trying to explain to herself. Despite years of police work under her belt, it was a case too complex even for her to solve.

Liz looked across to see that Nancy and Jack had vanished, something that happened almost every time the four of them got together. Whether they were having lunch in the Fish and Anchor or walking along the seafront, Nancy and Jack had a habit of disappearing in the blink of an eye, leaving Simon and Liz completely alone to face each other.

"So," Simon said, drumming his fingers on his

knees. "How's the shop?"

"It's good," she said with a nod. "Business is slow, but it's getting there. I'm having some supplier trouble at the moment. They're trying to squeeze my profit margins, but I'm standing my ground. How's the cheese?"

"Good," he replied. "Mum and Dad think they've found a shop down the coast who want to stock it, which would be great. More work, but it'd be worth it."

Liz looped Paddy's lead around her foot so she could drink more of the wine. When she had left Manchester in search of her new life on the South Coast, she had not expected to fall for a blond farmer with dimples who had a passion for making homemade cheese and ice cream, but that was exactly what had happened. And yet, she could not bring herself to talk to him in anything other than stilted, fragmented sentences.

A drunken man staggered towards them, sloshing his beer can over his shoulder, narrowly missing Paddy. Liz watched as the man swayed on the spot before clinging onto another man by his side, who looked less than happy about the situation.

Liz was about to jump in to defuse things before anything serious happened, but she stopped herself when she recognised the drunken man as Daniel Bishop, owner of The Sea Platter, Scarlet Cove's seafood restaurant. Since moving to town, it had become a regular spot for her and Nancy to have dinner and catch-up on the local gossip, and while there, Daniel had been nothing but polite and professional. She could barely bring herself to look into his eyes, not wanting him to know that she had seen him like this.

To her relief, Daniel apologised to the man, who begrudgingly accepted, perhaps because he also recognised Daniel from the popular restaurant. Liz was glad when he staggered away and out of sight.

"I've always thought people used this night as an excuse for getting drunk," Simon whispered, his shoulder leaning against Liz's, sending a hot spark through her cold arm. "You might want to make sure you're back home before midnight. That's when it starts to get rowdy."

"I'll bear that in mind," Liz whispered back, her lips twisting into a smile. "So, when does the ghost hunting start?"

"You actually believe the legend?"

"Not in the slightest. Do you?"

Simon considered his answer for a moment as he slurped his beer, the amber liquid wetting his pink lips in a way that made Liz instinctively lick her own.

"I'm not sure," Simon said, cocking his head to her, his rugged good looks softened in the crackling glow of one of the distant barrel fires. "Mum is convinced that it's true, but Dad isn't so sure. There are records that a man lived here with his wife, but their deaths aren't accounted for."

"There's nothing like an unexplained ending to get people's tongues wagging."

Simon chuckled as he drank his beer. Liz cast her eye over to the barbecue line. Nancy and Jack were queuing with empty hotdog buns in their hands. Nancy shot up two jolly thumbs over her bun; Liz pretended not to have seen.

"I think you're the first person I've spoken to all week who isn't definite that the legend is true," Liz said after another glug from her bag of wine. "I was starting to wonder if I was being too cynical."

"You must have seen a lot of nasty stuff in the

police."

Liz did not know why, but her mind instantly transported her back to the night her late husband, Lewis, had been shot. She felt the rain on her skin as though she was back there, and not two years in the future. The blood leaked from the gunshot wound and into the water, her hoarse cries drowned out by the pounding raindrops on the road around them.

She blinked hard. It had only been two years, but it felt like it had happened to another woman in another lifetime. His dying words had been '*be happy, Lizzy, please*', just as the ambulance had screeched to a halt next to them. Scarlet Cove was her life now, and she knew Lewis would have loved it here.

"Let's go for a walk," Liz said, suddenly jumping up as her mind snapped back to the present. "Paddy is getting restless."

"Sure," Simon said, finishing the last of his beer without questioning her. "Maybe we'll see some ghosts."

Liz laughed awkwardly, not wanting to admit that she had just seen a ghost from her own, not too distant, past.

With Paddy separating them, they broke away from the crowd and headed down one of the old stone corridors lining the courtyard. She looked into the crowd as the people of Scarlet Cove ate and drank, no doubt sharing their theories on what really happened here on that night hundreds of years ago.

They turned left, walls appearing on both sides of them. The inside of the castle had also been swathed in red light, unsettling her in a way she did not expect. She put it down to her flashback and not the ghost stories. Even so, she ran her fingers along the rough cold stone of the crumbling castle, sure she could hear the screams of the nobleman's wife as he brought the axe down on her neck.

"People say they've seen the wife up here," Simon said, a glimmer in his eyes. "Headless and all."

"How indecent of her."

"Nancy *swears* she saw her."

"I've heard that story too. I think Nancy might have had one too many glasses of wine that night."

"Probably." Simon laughed deeply, his gruff voice echoing off the walls, which seemed to be narrowing the deeper into the castle they walked.

A patch of the old ceiling vanished above them, forcing Liz to glance up. Milky clouds drifted lazily in front of the bright moon, her icy breath drifting up to join them. A shiver ran down her spine, prompting her to tuck her chin deeper into her tatty old scarf.

"I couldn't imagine living somewhere this big," Liz said, casting an eye back at the corridor as the darkness swallowed them up. "I'm more suited to my flat."

"Where did you live before?" Simon asked, the question rolling off his tongue so quickly that Liz was sure he had been waiting to ask it for weeks. "Before you came to Scarlet Cove?"

"Manchester."

"I know that much, but where? Did you have a flat up there?"

"Oh," Liz said, her previous glossy apartment nothing more than a foggy memory. "I had an apartment in one of those city blocks. All stainless steel and glass. No character. You know what it's like."

"I don't, actually," Simon said with an apologetic shrug. "I've lived -"

"In Scarlet Cove your whole life," Liz finished. "Didn't you leave to go to university? See some of the country before you settled here?"

"You don't need a degree to be a farmer."

"That's very true," she agreed. "Nor do you need to leave to know you've got a good home here."

"I have passion," he said with a soft smile. "That kept me here when everyone else ran off to explore."

Liz was sure she sensed a shred of resentment in his voice, long since suppressed and buried. She thought about her own time at university in Manchester when she had been a girl studying for her art degree. Those years had shaped her into the woman she was now, even if she had spent fifteen years being someone else entirely in the intermission.

"Look at me," Liz said, tossing her hand out as she directed Paddy towards a twisting stone staircase. "I ended up here, and I'm not even a native."

"I've spent so much time with you, and I still don't feel like I know you very much at all, Liz Jones," Simon said, his voice echoing as he trailed behind her. "I feel like my whole life is laid out to see and yet you're still a mystery."

"There's not much else to know," Liz said with

an uncomfortable laugh, fighting off the sudden urge to spill the intimate details of her loss. "I came here for a quieter life so I could live my dream of being a painter."

"And the bits in between?"

"Merely filler," she said, the urge vanishing as suddenly as it had sprung up. "I'm more interested in the here and now. Isn't that the only way to live?"

"I suppose," Simon said when they reached the top of the staircase. "Although, I don't think tonight is the night for living in the present, not when there are ghosts wandering around these corridors."

A small laugh escaped Liz as an icy breeze whistled down the corridor. They turned another corner and headed up three steps into one of the rooms. A glassless window frame stood grandly on the far side of the room, looking out over the town.

"This was the master bedroom," Simon said with a wink as he walked towards the window. "The legend says this is the room where the nobleman found his wife with the cook and –"

"Went on a beheading spree?"

"Exactly," he said with a deep chuckle. "You can see everything from up here. Look, there's your shop."

Liz joined Simon by the window and looked out into the dark, the twinkling lights of the town sloping towards the never-ending sea.

"It really is breath-taking up here," she said, her hot breath turning to condensation in the air. "I need to come up and paint this view during the day."

"I think you should," Simon said with a nod, turning to her with an easy smile. "You're a great painter."

"Thank you," she replied, the words catching in her throat as something bubbled up from her chest. "And you're a great cheese-maker."

He turned back to the view, his faint brows tensing tightly.

"Why Scarlet Cove?" he asked suddenly.

"Huh?"

"Why did you move to Scarlet Cove?"

"Should I not have done?"

"You know what I'm trying to say," he said, turning to her suddenly, squinting as though he was trying to look inside her for the answers he craved. "You could have gone anywhere for a new start.

There are plenty of places with pretty views to paint. Why *this* view?"

"Honestly?" Liz replied before clearing her throat, her fingers drifting up to scratch the side of her head. "I was walking past a charity shop one day, and one of the books in the window caught my attention. I went inside, picked it up, and I couldn't stop staring at the crystal blue sky and the harbour. I didn't put any more thought into it. I knew I wanted to leave Manchester, and in that moment, I knew I had found my new home. I didn't question it because I knew if I had, I would never have taken the leap. That was six months ago, and now here I am."

"You started your new life based on a book cover?" he asked, more than a little confused. "That's crazy, Liz!"

"It's as good a reason as any."

"What are you running from?" he asked before gulping so hard she would have sworn he was swallowing sawdust. "What happened in Manchester?"

Liz stared deep into Simon's eyes, wanting so badly to reveal herself to him, but unsure of how to do it. Had she not left that version of Liz behind? She was living in the present, and she could not think of anywhere she wanted to be more than next to the stunning view with the handsome farmer.

"Kiss me, Simon," she whispered, the words catching in the back of her throat. "I don't want to talk anymore. Just kiss me."

Simon nodded, a dumbfounded look spreading across his face. He grabbed the sides of her coat with trembling fingers, pulling her into him. Paddy's lead slipped from her fingers as she closed her eyes, two months of wondering about to reach a deserved conclusion.

She felt Simon's hot beer breath hit her nostrils, and it struck her that it was possibly the most masculine scent there was. She wondered what it would taste like to mix the beer and wine, sure she was about to find out.

Simon's lips brushed against hers, but a loud thud pulled them back just as quickly. Liz opened her eyes and turned to the door; the spell had been broken.

"*Paddy*," she muttered.

It seemed to take Simon longer to come to his

senses, so she headed for the door, leaving him by the window. It was not until she was running back down the spiral staircase towards the red lights that she heard Simon's footsteps behind her.

She stubbed her foot against something heavy in the dark, forcing her to stop in her tracks. The weight of it made her assume it was a piece of fallen stone, but it rolled away into the shadows like a football. Heart pounding in her chest, she looked down the corridor towards the red light, relief spreading through her when she heard Paddy's familiar bark. Leaving the solid ball behind, she set off towards the noise, skidding to a halt when she saw Paddy, and more importantly, saw what he was barking at.

"Oh my God," escaped her lips before she had time to think.

She scooped up the lead; her eyes transfixed on the scene in front of her. Just like on that night countless centuries ago, a headless body lay motionless on the stone tiles, blood trickling out of the neck into a far-reaching scarlet pool.

"*Liz?*" Simon's shaky voice echoed down the corridor. "I think you need to see this."

Unable to take her eyes away from the headless body, Liz walked backwards, the lead wrapped tightly around her hand as Paddy continued to bark. Gulping hard, she forced herself to turn around, her heart stopping once more when she saw Simon shining his bright phone screen on what she had kicked.

She had not kicked a ball, she had kicked a head, and not just anyone's, but the one belonging to Polly Spragg's boyfriend, Nathan.

Two

When Halloween rolled into town the next day, Liz was even less in the mood than usual. She had barely slept a wink, thanks to the head she had kicked. As she walked towards Coastline Cabaret to attend the Halloween party Nancy had insisted she go to, she was sure she could pass for a zombie, despite not having bothered with a costume.

She approached the bar on the seafront, an unpleasant wind whipping around her, dragging strands of red hair from the bun she had hastily made before leaving Paddy in the flat above her shop. She looked up at the bar's logo, its pink neon tubes glitching and fizzing in the dark as music and chatter floated through the closed door. Liz had assumed the Halloween party would have been cancelled, so she had been more than a little surprised when Nancy had called to inform her it was still going ahead as planned. Nancy had insisted nothing was to be gained from sitting at home, especially when none of them really knew Nathan that well. As Nancy had put it, his head would still be detached tomorrow.

Eager to get out of the cold, Liz yanked on the heavy door, the warmth consuming her in seconds. She unbuttoned her coat as she walked into the unfamiliar bar. When she had first arrived in the town, Nancy had said only old folks and tourists came to the bar, so Liz had not found a reason to visit, but it seemed the whole of Scarlet Cove was there to celebrate Halloween tonight. It quickly became apparent that she was one of the only ones not in costume.

The light of the neon sign continued inside, running along the ceiling in LED strips, casting pink shadows down on the padded benches and tables around the edge of the room. The colourful lights reminded her of the expensive cocktail bars back in Manchester, except they had been plucked out and put in a dated and gloomy old men's working club.

The bar stretched across the left side of the room, the wall behind it exposed redbrick. Wooden cubes of distressed wood jutted out from the brick, displaying the glass alcohol bottles. It did not seem like the most practical way to exhibit the drinks on offer, but it seemed to work because the bar was rammed. It was nothing like the Fish and Anchor, and did not seem to fit Scarlet Cove one bit.

Liz finished unbuttoning her coat and stepped forward, the old carpet sticky underfoot. She looked around at the sea of zombies, witches, and vampires, suddenly feeling exposed in her simple jumper and faded jeans.

"There you are!" Nancy pushed through the crowd, a grin plastered across her painted face. "I've been looking for you!"

Nancy had come as the bride of Frankenstein. She was wearing the traditional black beehive wig with silver Mallen streaks bolting up both sides, and a white gown that looked like an old nightie. She had painted her face a ghoulish shade of green, and inked her brows in black. Aside from her glasses, which looked completely out of place, she had not missed a detail.

"Where's your costume?" Nancy asked as she looked Liz up and down. "I told you it was fancy dress. People take it pretty seriously around here."

"I've been a little distracted," Liz said with a frown as she shrugged off her coat. "I'm sure people will understand."

"You poor thing," Nancy said, reaching out to rub Liz's arm. "I can't even imagine how you're feeling. You could have asked me for help with a costume. I have a whole box of stuff back at my place."

"Between you and me, I don't think I'll be sticking around for very long tonight," Liz said, looking around the room and noticing that more than a couple of people were suddenly whispering behind their hands now that they had spotted her. "I was giving my statement at the station for most of the night, but I knew if I didn't come, people would only talk."

"You *have* to stay," Nancy begged, grabbing Liz's hand in hers. "If only to take your mind off things. After a glass of wine, you'll be up there doing the '*Monster Mash*' with the rest of us! I'm sure someone will have some spare fake blood."

"As long as you keep it away from my neck," Liz said, her hand drifting up instinctively. "You're right about the wine, though. I think that's exactly what I need right now."

"That's the spirit!" Nancy exclaimed giddily, squeezing Liz's hand. "Come on. Let's go to the bar."

Liz tried to ignore the silence falling around them as they pushed through the crowd. She tried to tell herself it was not because she had been the one to find Nathan's beheaded body, but she would be naïve to think they were staring at her so intently because she had forgotten her costume.

"Two glasses of wine please, Patsy," Nancy asked when they got to the bar. "And a bag of nuts. I could eat a horse."

"Nice costume," the bartender replied. "Coming right up."

Liz watched Patsy grab two glasses from under the counter and fill them to the rim with wine, the traditional measures out of the window. Liz would have put her in her late-fifties from looking at her lined, discoloured hands, but the skin on her face looked taut, her brows too arched, and her lips overly plump. Liz guessed she had had a little help from a needle, something she had become accustomed to seeing back in the city. Her wiry hair was bleached blonde, with greying roots and was rolled up at the back, evoking the style of the nineteen-sixties. She dressed younger than her years, but Liz thought she made it work.

A hand closed tightly around Liz's shoulder, making her jump out of her skin. She grabbed the hand, immediately seizing the pressure points at the side of the wrist, her fingers digging into the hairy flesh.

"*Oww!*" Jack cried, his voice cracking. "*Jesus,* Liz!"

"Sorry," she mumbled, letting go quickly. "Old habit."

"She's a little – *on edge*," Nancy whispered as she adjusted her heavy wig. "Considering everything, I'd say it's lucky it was *just* your hand."

"Yeah, well, don't lose your head," Jack said, rubbing his hand where Liz had squeezed.

Liz arched a brow, wondering if Jack knew what he had just said. When he shook his head, his Frankenstein bolts bobbing up and down on his neck, she inhaled a calming breath before pinching between her brows. She should have stayed at home with Paddy. It was far too soon to be in public pretending she had not kicked a severed head twenty-four hours ago.

"Frankenstein and Mrs. Frankenstein," Patsy said as she slid the two glasses across the bar. "That's brilliant."

Nancy accepted her bag of nuts, a pleased grin stretching from ear to ear. Liz did not need to ask to know it was Nancy who had pulled together their costumes.

"*Technically*, it's Frankenstein's monster," Jack said, his eyes dancing over the different beer pumps behind the bar. "But everyone makes the same mistake, so I'll let you off."

Patsy stared blankly at Jack as she leaned against the bar, her plump lips pursing tightly.

"Beer?" she asked bluntly.

"Please," he replied sheepishly.

Patsy poured the pint and handed it over before Jack paid for their drinks. With her glass of wine clasped against her lips, Liz followed the couple through the crowd, which once again fell silent as it parted around her. She wondered if she should have come dressed as a leper.

"Is Simon here?" Liz asked hopefully. "I haven't spoken to him since it happened. The police interviewed us separately."

Nancy and Jack both glanced over their shoulders, not-so-subtle smiles on their green faces.

"He's around," Jack said, standing on tiptoe to look over the crowd. "Look for the scarecrow."

They wriggled through an enthusiastic group imitating the 'Thriller' dance on the crowded dance floor, every person in an elaborate costume. Aside from Patsy, Liz concluded that she was the only resident who had dared to turn up as herself. Considering the bags under her eyes and her un-brushed hair, she decided that was scary enough.

Liz was relieved when she spotted a scarecrow talking to Dracula. If she had not known what she was looking for, she would not have recognised the creature as Simon. Taking a huge gulp of wine, she broke away from Nancy and Jack before walking towards him.

"Nice costume."

"Liz!" the scarecrow exclaimed, Simon's familiar voice coming from the slit in the brown sack over his head. "I threw it together from stuff at the farm."

Simon pulled off his straw hat and slid the sack off his head, his face red and his dirty blond hair matted with sweat. She felt more at ease when he flashed his dimples.

"I came as myself," she said, motioning to her simple clothes. "*Boo!*"

"There's always next year," he said as he scratched at the straw poking out from his raggedy knitted jumper. "Truth be told, I wasn't even going to come, never mind dress up, but Mum and Dad forced me."

Simon nodded across the bar to Morticia and Gomez Addams, who were walking from side to side with their monster claws as Michael Jackson sang over the speakers. Ellie, Simon's little sister, was dancing between them dressed as Wednesday Addams. Her blonde hair had been spray-painted black and parted down the middle into tight plaits framing her tiny face.

"Part of me thinks I'm the only one bothered about what happened to Nathan," Liz said as they wandered towards the seats at the side of the room. "It's eating away at me."

"None of us really knew him all that well," Simon admitted with a shrug, echoing what Nancy had said over the phone. "He kept to himself. It's Polly I feel sorry for."

Liz's heart broke just thinking about what Polly must be going through. She had been through something similar with Lewis, but she guessed it was easier to grieve when you knew your spouse's head was still attached, even if they were lying in a morgue.

"I still feel weird about it," Simon admitted, turning to Liz as '*Thriller*' eased into The Backstreet Boys. "I used to nod to him at The Sea Platter, but I don't think we ever spoke."

"The Sea Platter?"

"He was the chef there," Simon said, before pausing and gulping hard. "You won't believe what people are saying."

"What?"

"They're saying they saw a ghost stalking the corridors with an axe after it happened."

Liz exhaled heavily before taking a deep gulp of her wine, practically inhaling half the glass in an instant.

"The poor guy was murdered by a living being in the *here* and *now*," she said firmly, irritation bubbling in her chest as the wine burned its way down to her stomach. "We owe the poor guy that much. If you chalk it down to a myth, we'll never find out the truth."

"We?"

"I meant the police," Liz corrected herself, her cheeks flushing. "The *police* will never find out the truth if the locals keep talking about the legend."

She smiled gently at Simon, not wanting to admit that she had spent most of the night going over everything she knew.

"We should find Nancy and Jack," Simon said as the music faded out. "I think the show's about to start."

"Show?"

By way of answer, Simon grabbed her hand and pulled her through the last of the crowd to where Nancy and Jack were defending two empty chairs. Liz and Simon slid into their places, turning to face the stage behind the suddenly cleared dance floor. The lights dimmed, and the chatter died down, a rumble of excitement echoing through the room.

Darkness descended, the only light coming from the pink strip lighting, which quickly turned red, staining the black walls, just as the floodlights had at the castle. A spotlight flashed into life, illuminating the red curtains as they began to part. A row of dancers appeared from the darkness, all of them in elaborate skull makeup and tuxedos. Applause scattered through the room as the well-dressed skeletons stared out into the dark sea of costumes. Even Liz found herself clapping along as the anticipation built.

The applause died down for a moment but immediately started again when a young woman walked onto the stage in a similar costume to the other skeletons. Her trousers had been ripped into shorts, and her shirt was open, revealing her chest. *'Time Warp'* from *'The Rocky Horror Picture Show'* started up, and the woman in the centre of the stage took the role of the narrator, the dancers behind her doing as instructed. It only took seconds for people, including Nancy and Jack, to fill up the dance floor once again.

Liz sipped her wine, her foot tapping along in time to the music. She glanced at Simon, who was mouthing the words, his hips wiggling in the chair. Smiling to herself, she rested her head on his shoulder, knowing the wine had already loosened her up. When Simon's arm snaked around her shoulders, she flinched a little, but relaxed into his side; it felt right.

The song finished, and there was a gap of silence before the next one started. If it had not been for that tiny blip of nothingness, Liz and the rest of the town might not have heard the doors burst open. The force of the sound caused everyone to suddenly shift in their chairs to stare at the door. *'The Monster Mash'* started up, but the dancers and the girl at the front just stood and stared. Liz half-stood up and looked over the crowd, her heart skipping a beat when she saw Polly striding into the bar, makeup streaked down her face, her usual peroxide beehive deflated and sagging at the side of her head. She pushed through the crowd with such intent, it was obvious to everyone that she was not there to enjoy the party.

The singer tried to catch up with the song as the dancers bopped limply behind her. With the intensity of a wild animal, the usually bubbly hairdresser burst through the stunned crowd and yanked the singer down off the stage with one swift tug. A gasp escaped Liz's lips, as well as those of every other person who was staring in disbelief. The music suddenly stopped as the dancers watched helplessly. The crowd parted in a circle around Polly and the singer, who was on the floor after her fall from the high stage.

"I *knew* something was going on with you and Nathan," Polly screeched, her voice so high Liz was sure Paddy would be howling back at the flat. "I *knew* it!"

"Wha-" the woman mumbled as she forced herself up to her feet. "You're insane!"

"Don't you *dare* try to deny it!" Polly screeched,

her foot stomping as her fists clenched tightly by her sides. "I saw the messages on his phone just before - just before it happened."

Polly took a step towards the woman, who was looking feebly around the thick crowd, a disbelieving, awkward smile on her face. Just from the look in the singer's eyes, Liz knew Polly was on to something.

"Who's that?" Liz whispered to Simon as she craned her neck above the stage.

"Misty Rivers. She's been performing here for a while."

Misty flattened down her black shoulder-length hair as she stared at Polly, her mouth opening but no sound forming between her lips.

"You're not even *trying* to deny it!" Polly screamed even louder, causing Misty to jump back. "Girls like you make me *sick*!"

They stood in the circle for what felt like a lifetime, like two alley cats getting ready to pounce and fight. Nobody rushed forward to part the women, probably so stunned they were frozen to the spot like Liz.

"How could you do this?" Polly yelled, suddenly

launching forward and grabbing a fistful of Misty's hair. "You *stupid* little-"

Before Polly could finish her sentence, a plump, balding, bespectacled man pushed through the crowd.

"What are you *doing*?" he cried, staring at Polly, his disbelieving eyes wide behind his magnifying spectacles. "Let *go* of her!"

"Derrick, it's fine," Misty winced, her fingers wrapped around Polly's wrist, which still had a fistful of her hair entangled in it. "She's probably just inhaled too many peroxide fumes."

Polly stared at the entertainer for a moment; her insult seemed to be the straw to break the camel's back. She let out a tribal screech, which echoed into the darkest corners of the bar. Liz swiftly jumped up, but before she could rush over to part the women, the balding man dragged the hairdresser away from the cowering singer.

"*Enough!*" he yelled, standing between the women, his wide stomach blocking Misty completely from Liz's view. "You've *ruined* the show for everyone! Just *leave!*"

Polly stumbled back, her eyes trained on Misty,

who remained firmly behind the man. Polly seemed to be considering whether it was worth taking another shot, but decided against it, much to Liz's relief. She turned on her heels and bolted back through the crowd, slamming the door just as she had only minutes ago. Silence remained in the club as the dancers climbed down from the stage to comfort Misty. Liz left Simon's side and walked over to Nancy and Jack, who had watched the whole ordeal unravel from the side-lines.

"She's just jealous of your talent," said the man who Liz had heard Misty call Derrick. "Let's go and get you cleaned up. The show *must* go on."

Misty nodded quickly, her chin raised to the ceiling. She scanned the crowd, her eyes meeting Liz's briefly.

"You heard the man," she cried, shrugging off Derrick before clapping her hands together. "The show *must* go on. You came here to watch me perform, and that's what's going to happen. Girls, back on stage. Give the people what they want while I freshen up."

Misty let herself be led through the crowd by Derrick, his arm clamped tightly around her shoulder. The dancers climbed back up onto the stage, and *The Monster Mash* started from the beginning. They began dancing with the same bewildered and confused looks as the people watching them. Nancy turned to Liz, her jaw slack.

"Just when you thought things couldn't get any more dramatic," Nancy whispered, an excited smile pricking the corners of her mouth. "Nathan and Misty? Who would have known? Did you know about this, Jack?"

"I didn't know the fella," Jack admitted, holding his hands up. "I never thought he was a good fit for Polly, but that was none of my business."

Liz remembered thinking the same thing when she had met Nathan outside the castle less than an hour before meeting his head in the dark corridor.

"Poor Polly," Simon said, appearing behind Liz as the crowd started to disperse. "I wouldn't have thought she could get that angry. She's always seemed so -"

"Sweet," Nancy finished.

"Grief can do strange things to people," Liz said, almost to herself. "How long were Polly and Nathan together?"

"Not long," Nancy said, her eyes narrowing as she dug through her memory. "I think they got together after me and Jack, so less than a year."

"Last night was the first time I saw them together," Liz thought aloud, her finger tapping on her chin. "I see Polly all the time."

"Maybe he was too busy with his side piece," Simon whispered, his hands grabbing Liz's shoulders from behind. "I hope she's okay."

"She won't be," Liz said bluntly, shrugging off Simon's hands. "It's bad enough that her boyfriend died like he did, but to find out he was cheating will have added a knife in her back to join the one in her heart." Liz looked in the direction Misty and Derrick had headed, spotting an opening to a corridor. "I'll be right back."

After passing her wine glass to Nancy, Liz pushed through the crowd, some of whom were half-heartedly trying to resume their dancing. She slipped down the dark corridor unseen, stopping when she came to a door with Misty's name stuck to a glittery gold star. It looked like something that had been made in a high school art project.

Liz knocked on the door, and was surprised

when she heard Misty call "*Come in.*"

Liz entered the dressing room, the sickly scent of sweet perfume knotting her stomach. Misty stared at herself in a mirror surrounded by soft vanity lights. She dabbed under her eyes with a tissue, her intricate skull makeup swirling into a grey mess.

Half a dozen pictures had been stuck to the edge of the mirror. A gorgeous woman with porcelain white skin jumped out from the professional headshots, her curled jet-black hair bringing to mind a 1940s burlesque dancer. Liz assumed it was the same woman in the chair, who was still strikingly beautiful, even behind the inky makeup.

"You're not Derrick," Misty said bluntly when she spotted Liz in the glowing reflection. "Can I help you?"

Liz applied her friendliest interview smile, which she had honed during her years in the force. It had not taken her long in her early days to realise that it was easier to pry information with a smile than a scowl.

"I just wanted to check you were okay," Liz said softly in a maternal voice that felt foreign to her. "That was quite a scene out there."

"I'm fine," she snapped, sniffling one last time before picking up a makeup brush and dipping it into a black pot of grease paint. "Who are you? You're not one of the regulars."

"This is my first time here," Liz replied, taking Misty's question as permission to approach. "I only moved here a few months ago."

"Oh," Misty said as she began to re-trace the outline of the skull, her eyes darting up and down Liz. "What's your costume?"

"I'm not wearing one."

"Oh," she said again, her eyes widening as she focused in on her own face. "I thought you'd come as a fashion victim."

Liz looked down at her khaki jumper and faded jeans, wondering if she really looked that bad, not that she cared either way. Since moving to Scarlet Cove, she rarely wore anything she was not happy to have covered in paint splatters.

"I suppose you want to know if Polly was telling the truth?" Misty said flatly as she coloured in the missing spaces under her eyes. "That's why you're really here."

Liz's smile faltered as she met the woman's dark

eyes in the mirror. Despite being beautiful, she came across as cold, like a perfect face carved from a slab of white marble.

"It's not really any of my business," Liz said, not wanting to give any of her intentions away.

"It's true," Misty admitted, her voice devoid of emotion. "He was going to break up with that bimbo."

"Polly is a nice woman."

"Is that her name?" Misty asked with a shrug. "Mutton dressed as lamb. Nathan never loved her, but when you're living with someone, it isn't that easy. After that performance out there, the whole town will see how unstable she is."

Liz let her smile fade away. She narrowed her eyes on the beautiful woman as she finished touching up her makeup, not caring if it was obvious that she had taken an instant dislike to the performer.

"She tried to own him," she continued. "He was a free spirit. He wanted someone more exciting, someone who didn't want to keep him in a box. She was holding him back."

"Is that an excuse for breaking a young woman's

heart?" Liz asked, crossing her arms.

"It's her own fault for being so fragile," Misty said with a roll of her eyes. "Hearts are broken, and people die. It's part of life. I am upset that Nathan is dead. I liked the guy, but I'm not going to waste my life mourning, especially when I have a show to do. Speaking of which, I need to get back out there. Those dimwit dancers won't keep them distracted for long. The people came to see the *star* of the show, and that's what they're going to get. I'll make that stupid hairdresser pay if she's lost me this job."

Liz did not feel the need to say another word. She knew nothing further could be gained from their conversation, and if she stayed, she was not sure she could hold her tongue.

Leaving Misty to keep admiring herself in the soft glow of the mirror, Liz made her way back to her friends. Nancy handed Liz her wine, which she drained in seconds.

"Where've you been?" Nancy asked, her lips pursed and arms crossed.

"Bathroom."

"The toilet is on the other side," Nancy said, nodding at the illuminated sign near the bar. "Are you investigating?"

"Why would you think that?" Liz replied, knowing her tone was a little too defensive. "I'm going to get another glass of wine. Same again for everyone else?"

"Sure," they replied in unison.

After another round of drinks, they made their way to the door. Despite Misty's quick reappearance on the stage, the club had half emptied since Polly's outburst. After Jack and Nancy linked arms and bid them goodnight, Simon and Liz hung back underneath the flickering pink neon sign.

"So," Simon said, looking down at his shoes. "I was wondering if you'd like to come back to the farm for a coffee? The night is still young, and my parents are still in there with Ellie."

Liz had wanted to spend the rest of her evening painting at her flat, but the hopeful look in Simon's eyes convinced her to ditch her plans; she could paint tomorrow.

"Coffee sounds good," she said, earning a smile from Simon that made the butterflies in her stomach resurface. "Lead the way, scarecrow."

The walk up to Simon's farm was a long one,

but with Simon by her side, the time passed quickly. They chatted about everything and nothing, arm in arm as they walked along the dirt track to the old farm.

"I only have instant coffee," Simon said as he unhooked the large metal gate blocking off the farm from passing visitors. "I hope that's okay."

"It's what I drink at home," she said, stepping over a large puddle as she followed him through. "I've found I'm more of a tea drinker since moving here."

They relinked arms as they set off towards the dark farmhouse. Simon stopped suddenly in his tracks, forcing Liz to halt by his side. She stared ahead at the farmhouse, something white glowing in the dark on the doorstep. They looked at each other, and then back to the motionless ethereal figure. For one ridiculous moment, Liz's first thought was that it was the headless wife from the castle. After a shake of her head, she yanked on Simon's arm, and they approached the figure.

When they were metres away, Liz could see that it was a woman in a white wedding dress. On any other night, she might have been surprised to see someone dressed as a bride at this time of night, but since it was Halloween, the sight did not seem so unexpected, and yet, it did not quite feel right. The dress was too clean and perfect, and the woman wearing it was sobbing into her hands, not even knowing that she was being watched.

Liz's foot accidentally struck a small stone, bouncing it towards the doubled-over woman with a rattle. The bride squinted into the dark, her cheeks streaked with mascara.

"Simon?" the woman croaked.

"*Natasha?*" Simon replied, his voice unsteady and eyes wide. "W-what are you doing here?"

Simon and Natasha stared at each other for what felt like an eternity. Liz had no idea what was happening, but she pulled her arm away from Simon's and took a small step back.

The woman jolted up and ran towards Simon, her puffy dress floating behind her in the night breeze. She wrapped her arms tightly around his neck and sobbed into his shoulder. Simon rested a hand on the woman's back and patted softly.

"Oh, Simon," she sobbed. "I couldn't go through with it. I couldn't marry him. I didn't know where else to go."

"I should go," Liz said faintly.

She waited for Simon to tell her to stay, but she was met with silence. Deciding she was not going to stay where she was not wanted, she headed back to the gate. Baffled and confused, she wandered back down to Scarlet Cove, leaving the farmer and the bride to hug in the dark.

Three

Liz bolted up in bed the next morning, her dreams having been haunted by headless men and ghostly brides. She pushed her frizzy hair out of her eyes as she stared at Paddy who gazed back up at her with a tilted head from the side of the bed.

She grabbed her phone, squinting at the time in the murky darkness, the sun barely in the sky yet.

She had three notifications. The first was a text from her friend and fellow detective, Miles, who was letting her know the news of the beheading had made its way up to the station in Manchester. The second was a text from Nancy asking how things had gone with Simon. The third was letting her know her mobile phone bill was due now that it was the first of November. There was nothing from Simon.

Liz tossed back the covers and changed from her pyjamas into a thick jumper and dark blue jeans, the cold nipping at her in between. She felt the white radiator under her small bedroom window, but it had not yet kicked in.

"Again?" she mumbled with a sigh, making a mental note to call her landlord, Bob Slinger, about the faulty boiler. "Are you hungry, boy?"

After feeding Paddy and letting him do his morning business in the yard behind her shop, she wrapped a burgundy scarf around her neck and slipped her hands into a pair of mittens. She had an hour until the shop needed to open, so she set off towards Tidal Trinkets on the seafront.

The wind was stronger than she had experienced before in Scarlet Cove, and the waves were unforgiving as they spat their spray over the sea wall, the small beach below completely hidden. Dark clouds circled above, making the early morning sun nothing more than a grey blur in the murky sky. Even without the clouds, Liz could smell rain was on the way.

She arrived at the shop at the same time as the owner, Sylvia, who was dressed in a similar fashion to Liz. She hung back by the sea wall and waited for the petite woman to fully open the shop. When she flicked the lights on and perched on her stool behind the counter, Liz approached.

Sylvia was a little woman in her early sixties. She had an open, caring face, and a talent for crafts, which she sold in her shop. Since opening, Sylvia had made Liz's shop her supplier of choice, and the two women had bonded over their shared creativity.

"Hello, Liz," Sylvia smiled as she entered. "How are you, my dear? Bit early, isn't it?"

"Chilly too," Liz said, rubbing her mittens together in the cold shop. "My radiator is on the blink."

"If you've come for some warmth, it will be a while until mine kicks in. Customers don't start showing up for another hour or so, but you know I like to come down here and read my novellas. The peace and quiet is just what I need."

The shop was small and modest like most of the others in town, but had more charm than any other souvenir shop Liz had ever visited. Authenticity oozed from the shelves, Sylvia's beautiful handmade knick-knacks begging to be bought. Liz had already bought a shell covered jewellery box and some necklaces to go with it, not that she had found a reason to wear them yet.

"I hope you don't mind me interrupting your reading time," Liz said, edging closer to the counter as she unravelled her scarf. "I wanted to talk to you about Polly."

"I've called in a few times, but she's not being co-operative," Sylvia said with a heavy sigh as she plucked off her gloves finger by finger. "She says she's fine, but my granddaughter is an awful liar."

Sylvia tossed her gloves onto the counter before plucking a dated and dog-eared romance novella from her bag. Liz caught a glimpse of a bare-chested man with a woman draped across his arm on the cover, but Sylvia quickly turned the book upside down.

"I was thinking I might pop by and visit her," Liz said hopefully. "I just want to make sure she's okay, but I'm not quite sure where she lives."

"I think seeing a familiar face other than me will be good for her," Sylvia agreed with a nod. "I always thought she came to Scarlet Cove to look after me, but then she got involved with that Nathan boy. I knew he was trouble from the minute I saw him."

"Did you know much about Nathan?"

"I don't even think Polly did," Sylvia said, sighing as she ran her finger along the tattered back cover. "Not really, anyway. I think she just projected her dream man onto him. Bit of a blank page. Not much personality, if you get what I'm saying. Polly is a sweet girl, but she's got a head full of dreams. She gets carried away. She's impulsive."

"How so?"

"Well, she moved to Scarlet Cove on a whim," Sylvia said. "It's nice to have my only granddaughter close by, but she came here on holiday a couple of years ago and never left. She had a top job back in Essex, but she left it behind to start her own salon here. It's worked out for her, but I suppose she's always been lucky like that. Some people just always land on their feet, but that luck had to run out. She's getting her share all in one dose, but life can be cruel like that."

"I know how she feels."

"You do?" Sylvia asked, her kind eyes looking deep into Liz's. "Well, if you want to try and cheer her up, she lives a few doors down from the Fisherman's Rest B&B. Number twenty-three. She'll probably be awake. She's always been an early riser, just like me."

"Thank you," Liz said, making a mental note of the address. "Enjoy the rest of your book."

"Before you go," Sylvia reached into her handbag and pulled out a metal tin. "Can you give this to Polly? She loves salted caramel fudge."

Liz took the box from Sylvia with a promise to pass it on. She left the shop, wrapped the scarf back around her head, and set off towards the Fisherman's Rest B&B. Just as she suspected, tiny droplets of water fell from the heavy clouds above.

***

WITH THE FUDGE IN ONE HAND AND A

bunch of flowers from the corner shop in the other, Liz walked up the garden path leading to Polly's small house near the B&B. She knocked loudly on the door, knowing it was far too early for visitors.

"*Polly?*" she called through the wood. "It's Liz. Are you up?"

Liz heard shuffling on the other side of the door, so she pushed forward a sympathetic smile from behind the flowers. Polly opened the door and squinted through the gap, the dim light appearing to burn her eyes.

"*Liz?*" she croaked, as though she had been asleep. "What a surprise. Come in."

Polly opened the door and shuffled back down the hallway, the tie from her dressing gown trailing behind. Liz followed her into the front room, which was decorated just as she would have expected. Every accessory was either hot pink or glittery and silver. The chimney breast had been papered in pink and white zebra print, and a shiny black miniature chandelier hung from the white textured ceiling, despite the room being too small to warrant it. Pizza boxes were stacked up on the glass coffee table as though they were all Polly had been living on over the last couple of days.

"Sorry about the mess," Polly said as she curled up in the corner of the white leather couch, a pink cushion clutched to her chest. "I usually keep it so clean."

"No need to apologise," Liz said, sitting next to Polly on the squeaky couch. "You should see my place."

Polly could barely raise a smile. She looked nothing like the bubbly woman Liz had loved from the moment she had met her in the hair salon. Instead of her usual makeup covered face and tanned skin, she was completely bare and pale, her white hair in a loose ponytail at the side. She looked as though the ink in the printer was just about to run out and she was the final faint sheet.

"I've just come from your gran's shop," Liz said, offering the tin of fudge. "She asked me to give you this. The flowers are from me."

Polly accepted both gifts, staring at them for a second before moving them to the side table as though it was a game of pass the parcel.

"Thank you," Polly said, barely above a whisper. "Salted caramel fudge is my favourite."

The words sounded like they were leaving Polly's mouth automatically, reminding Liz of an answering machine message.

"How are you?" Liz asked after another awkward silence, knowing the question was a useless one.

"I'm great," she said, her tone unusually sarcastic. "My boyfriend had his head chopped off after I found out he was cheating on me."

Liz reached out to grab Polly's hand, which seemed to take the hairdresser by surprise. Their eyes met, and Liz tried to convey that she understood part of what Polly was going through. The only reason she did not say the words out loud was because she was not sure bringing up her own loss would make things any better.

"I don't know what I'm more upset about," Polly said, suddenly turning to meet Liz's eyes. "The fact he's dead, or the fact he was cheating on me. That's a horrible thing to say, isn't it?"

"No," Liz said, squeezing her hand hard. "You've been through a lot. There are no rules to this process. You just have to get through it one day at a time."

Polly smiled and nodded, a silent tear trickling

down her pale cheek.

"Is that your police training kicking in?" Polly asked.

"No," she replied firmly. "I'm speaking from experience. Not the cheating part, but I've been there when it comes to losing someone you love."

"What do you mean?"

Liz almost changed the subject, but the words were on the tip of her tongue, and she was not sure if she could swallow them down.

"My husband died in Manchester," she started, pausing to take a deep breath. "It's been two years, almost three now. He was an officer too. We were working on a case together, and something went wrong. He got caught in the path of a bullet that wasn't even meant for him. It killed him. He died on the scene."

"Liz," Polly said, raising her hand to her mouth. "I had no idea. I'm so sorry."

"Why would you know? I came here for a fresh start. It's what he would have wanted. It might seem odd, but I grieved very quickly because I knew he would have hated me to be stuck there. He was all about living in the present and not worrying about things you can't control. I knew there was nothing I could do to bring him back, and I just had to accept that."

"I think if I could bring him back, I'd kill him myself," Polly said, letting go of Liz's hand and shuffling even further into the corner. "My love turned to hatred the second I saw the message from Misty on his phone. He dropped it at the castle, so I picked it up to give it to him. The screen lit up. I saw the message from that *tramp*. It said something like: '*can't wait to see you tonight. Text me when the bimbo has fallen asleep*'. It had tons of kisses at the end. He didn't even try to deny it. He just took his phone and walked away. I tried to follow him, to find out what was happening, but I couldn't find him. And then –"

"Do you know who could have done this?" Liz asked firmly, edging forward. "Did Nathan have any enemies?"

"It *must* be Misty," Polly said surely, not hiding her disdain. "She was swanning around that damn bar like nothing had happened. She didn't care at all. He probably didn't have enough money to keep up with her and her stupid dreams of getting out of here. She has a reputation."

"A reputation?" Liz coaxed.

"She's a diva," Polly said through a strained laugh. "Probably a gold digger too. I bet she's the type of woman who uses men for whatever she can get out of them. She wouldn't have got a penny from Nathan. I had to lend him money most weeks, and I bet he was spending it on *her*. How did I not see it, Liz? Why did I let this happen?"

"You didn't make him cheat on you."

"Didn't I?" Polly replied, sniffling hard. "What if I'm not enough? What if I was too annoying? He always said he liked my quirks, but what if he was just with me to have a roof over his head?"

Liz did not tell Polly her fears echoed something Misty had said. Instead, she grabbed her hand and squeezed again, hoping her sympathy comforted her.

"So, you don't know anyone else who had it in for Nathan?"

"It *must* be her," Polly repeated, nodding her head. "Maybe he told her he wanted to be with me? Maybe he realised she was one of *those* girls?"

Liz let Polly's hand slip out of hers again. Polly crammed the ends of her fingers into her mouth and chomped down on her bare nails, which looked like her usual press-on nails had recently been ripped off. Liz knew all too well that mood swings were part of the process, and she was not about to deny Polly that. She watched as the hairdresser gnawed her nails like a hungry animal. She noticed a deep cut on the side of her hand, and it looked quite fresh.

"I cut my hand on the scissors at the salon," Polly said when she noticed Liz staring. "Grandma says I'm the clumsiest person she knows."

Liz did not ask any more questions. She did not like where her imagination was taking her. She left Polly with her salted caramel fudge and flowers before walking across town to her shop. After opening up, she sat behind the counter and pulled out her sketchpad as Paddy curled up at her feet.

She flicked past a crude drawing of the front of her shop that she had sketched out last week, landing on a fresh page. With a dark pencil, she wrote 'Nathan' in the centre and encased it in a bubble. She drew two lines away from his name, adding 'Misty Rivers' to the end of one, and 'Polly Spragg' to the other.

Four

"I heard about your little visit to see Polly yesterday," Nancy said with a raised eyebrow as they wandered down the seafront with Paddy. "Jack heard someone talking about it in the pub."

"I just wanted to check that she was okay," Liz said casually, wishing she had asked Sylvia to keep the news of her visit to herself. "Someone needs to."

Paddy pulled them towards the sea wall before cocking his leg. Liz looked out across the thrashing waves, hoping Nancy would drop the subject and get back to complaining about her boss at the gallery where she worked.

"I know you're investigating," Nancy continued, tickling Liz in the ribs. "You can tell me. I might be able to help."

"I'm just-"

"Liz Jones!" Nancy cried, stopping her mid-sentence. "You can't fool me. Spit it out. Tell me!"

Paddy finished relieving himself, turning his attention to a seagull a couple of steps ahead. He ran forward, yanking on Liz's arm. She pulled him back as they set off walking again.

"Fine," Liz said firmly, squinting into the distance towards The Sea Platter. "I wanted to see if Polly knew anything. I found the body-"

"And the head," Nancy jumped in.

"*And* the head," Liz continued. "I feel compelled to at least ask some follow-up questions."

An icy gust of wind washed down the seafront, fluttering their hair from side to side.

"I want to help," Nancy said with a resolute

nod. "You jumped into harm's way when you figured out who killed poor Frank. Two heads will be better than one."

"I'm *not* investigating," Liz insisted, her teeth chattering. "And what makes you think things will be less dangerous if you're helping?"

"Because I'm your friend, and I happen to know a lot about this little town," Nancy said smugly. "You could learn a lot from me, Detective."

"*Retired* detective," Liz reminded her.

With a friendly roll of her eyes, Nancy linked her arm through Liz's as they carried on along the front, following Paddy as he sniffed the pavement like a police dog in an airport.

A stray cat caught Paddy's attention, dragging them across the road to the business side of the street. The cat darted past The Sea Platter, almost knocking a man off his feet as he carried empty crates in his arms. He dropped the crates, revealing his flushed face.

"Simon?" Liz said suddenly, her tongue feeling like it was quickly swelling in her mouth.

"Liz," Simon replied as he steadied the crates, his cheeks reddening more. "How are you?"

Liz stared at him for a moment, wondering what sort of question it was to ask after what had happened at the farmhouse. She had desperately wanted to know who the woman was and why she had turned up on Simon's doorstep in a wedding dress, but Simon had not called, and she was not about to make the first move.

"Can we talk?" Simon asked, glancing at Nancy.

"Sure," Liz said, pulling Nancy closer into her side. "About what?"

Nancy tried to wriggle away, but Liz clung onto her. Simon sighed as a gust of wind rustled his short hair, looking as though he wanted the breeze to sweep him away.

"I feel like I should explain," Simon started. "I – "

"You don't need to explain anything to me," Liz said suddenly. "It's really none of my business."

"Natasha is a –" Simon broke off, glancing down at his shoes with furrowed brows. "It's complicated."

"Like I said, it's none of my business."

Simon's eyes drifted up to meet hers. They were filled with sadness, as though he was about to break up with her, even though they were never an official couple.

"We need to go," Liz said quickly, desperate to save herself the embarrassment. "See you around."

Liz dropped her head and hurried around Simon, dragging Nancy and Paddy with her. As they passed Tidal Trinkets, she dared to look back, disappointed when she saw Simon climbing into his car. Had she expected him to follow?

"You know about Natasha?" Nancy asked, her voice small. "I was going to mention something, but I didn't know how much you knew."

"I don't know anything," Liz said quickly. "I went to the farmhouse with Simon after the party, and there she was, sitting on his doorstep. It paints its own picture, doesn't it?"

"Oh, Liz," Nancy said with a heavy sigh. "Why didn't you mention something?"

"Because I didn't want pity."

"It's not what it seems," Nancy said, her voice as unsure as Simon's had been. "Not really."

They walked in silence for almost a full minute, neither of them speaking until they passed the harbour. Nancy pulled her towards a bench, and she reluctantly sat down, unclipping Paddy's lead extension so he could wander around them.

"I thought we'd seen the last of Natasha," Nancy started, her brows tensing behind her thick-rimmed glasses. "It's been so long."

Liz chewed the inside of her cheek, part of her not wanting to hear any more. It almost seemed easier to draw a line under things with Simon if she only had half a picture to work from, but her own curiosity stopped her from cutting Nancy off.

"It must have been fifteen years," Nancy said as the wind whistled around them. "Doesn't feel that long ago when you think about it. One minute you're eighteen, the next you're thirty-four."

"Is she an ex-girlfriend?" Liz asked bluntly.

"It *was* fifteen years ago," Nancy repeated. "We've all known each other since we were kids. It's a small town. Jack and Simon have been friends for as long as I can remember, but I didn't really join their thing until I started dating Jack last year. I never really knew Natasha all that much, if I'm being honest. She always thought she was better than this place, that's why I was so surprised to hear she'd boomeranged back. It's not like she still has family here. They left years ago."

"Well, she came back for some reason," Liz said. "She came back for Simon."

"They were only together for two years," Nancy said with a forced laugh as she shook her head. "It wasn't some great romance. They were kids. They broke it off when they were eighteen. Natasha went to university, and Simon didn't. They tried the long-distance thing for a while, but it just fizzled out. She never came back."

"Until now."

Nancy rested her head on Liz's shoulder. "I'm sure it's not like it seems. Simon isn't like that."

Liz knew deep down that Simon was not a bad person, but she knew love, especially long-held love, could change a person's behaviour in the blink of an eye.

"Have they not seen each other since then?" Liz asked, her curiosity in the subject piqued. "Fifteen years is a long time to leave it before turning up."

"I don't think so," Nancy said, her face scrunching up. "Simon never mentioned it."

"But they could have?"

"Maybe," Nancy admitted. "But I doubt it. He's

never spoken about her. I'd forgotten she even existed!"

"It doesn't mean Simon had," Liz said. "To turn up in a wedding dress like that is just –"

"A wedding dress?" Nancy jumped in. "Jack left that part out. You don't think she –"

"Ran away from her wedding to be with Simon?" Liz finished. "It looked too expensive to just be a Halloween costume."

They stared out at the road as Paddy wandered past, his nose grazing the ground. Liz glanced back towards The Sea Platter; Simon's car had gone.

"Have you seen her?" Liz asked.

"Not since she's been back," Nancy said as she pulled her phone from her pocket. "Jack went up to the farm last night to hang out with Simon. He said she looked like she was making herself at home."

"She's still there?" Liz mumbled, her eyes flickering as she imagined the runaway bride wandering around the farmhouse in Simon's shirts and laughing with Simon's parents. "I guess she's sticking around."

"I'm sorry, Liz," Nancy said as she stood up, tucking her phone back into her pocket. "I need to go. It's date night with Jack. I can cancel if you need me to? I feel bad leaving you like this."

"I'm fine," Liz lied, pushing forward a smile. "Nothing was really happening with me and Simon, was it? We never even kissed."

Nancy looked as though she was about to say, '*but you wanted to*', but she stopped herself. They hugged their goodbyes, Nancy squeezing even tighter than usual before she scurried off down the seafront, darting down a back alley and out of view.

"Come on, boy," Liz said as she reattached Paddy's extendable lead. "Let's go home."

As they passed The Sea Platter, Liz glanced through the window. She spotted Daniel setting tables, but much like his drunken appearance at the castle on the night of the beheading, he looked less like his professional self and a little worse for wear. Even through the window, Liz could see the bags under his eyes. Remembering what Simon had said about Nathan working at the restaurant, Liz tied Paddy's lead around a lamppost before heading into the warm interior.

"Table for one, Liz?" he asked, forcing a polite tone, but clearly exhausted. "It's a bit quiet today.

The weather is keeping the tourists away."

Liz looked around the restaurant, which was unusually empty compared to what she had seen on her regular visits with Nancy. She glanced at the clock, surprised that it was almost five in the evening.

"I can't stay," she said, noticing his instant disappointment. "I was just wondering if I could ask you some questions."

"Questions?" he replied, letting go of the cutlery to cross his arms. "About what?"

Liz wondered if she could dance around the subject, but from the firm look in the man's tired eyes, it seemed he knew what she was about to say.

"It's about Nathan," she said with an unsure smile, remembering how much easier it was to question people when she could flash them her police badge. "I heard that he was a chef here?"

"I've already answered the police's questions more than once," he said quickly, dropping his arms, and turning to start setting another table. "If you don't mind, I have a family booked in, and they'll be here any minute."

"I just wanted to know what might have

happened to him," Liz said, running around the table so they were face to face again. "I was the one to find him, and nobody seems to know much about him."

"I don't know any more than you do," he said dismissively, his jaw tightening. "It's not like we were friends. He was my employee. I really do need to get to work. I can't afford not to, especially now that I'm juggling the front of house and the kitchen."

"Surely you can't do both jobs at once?" Liz asked, arching a brow. "Maybe you should hire another chef?"

"With what money?" he snapped, suddenly straightening up to stare at Liz as though she was the source of all his problems. "I could barely afford Nathan as it was. It's coming up to the winter season. People don't come here when it's like this. I usually save up, but the summer wasn't much better. It doesn't help that the fish prices keep going up."

"The fish?" Liz said, her brow crinkling. "Have you spoke to Chris about this? Surely he'll-"

Before Liz could finish her sentence, and as though he had known he was being spoken about,

Christopher Monroe, the owner of the harbour, strode into the restaurant, the collar of his trench coat turned up to his jaw. He scanned the empty restaurant, his eyes lighting up when they landed on Liz.

"Elizabeth," Christopher said with a tight smile. "A pleasure as always."

As though he could tell they were in the middle of a conversation, Christopher sat at his usual table by the window. Liz recognised it as the one she had sat at with him on their failed '*date*' when she had first moved to Scarlet Cove.

"How are you managing to do everything yourself?" Liz asked quietly, one eye trained on Christopher as he glanced over the menu. "It can't be easy for you."

"It's not," Daniel said, glancing over his shoulder in Christopher's direction. "Especially since *someone* keeps jacking up the price of fish!"

"Was that directed at me?" Christopher asked, laying the menu on the table to smooth down his pale blond hair. "It's just inflation, my friend. A by-product of business."

"Well, I won't have a business left if the season

keeps on like this." Daniel hurried behind the small bar in the corner and flicked on the music. "We're in for a long winter."

"Aren't you a little upset that he's not here?" Liz asked, following him across the restaurant, desperate to gauge Daniel's reaction to his chef's murder. "I know you said you weren't friends, but you must have been a little close to him working here."

"I don't have time for this," Daniel snapped finally. "I've told you, I'm busy. Go to the police if you have any questions."

Liz stared at the man, shocked by his tone. She abandoned plans to move her questioning onto the night at the castle, his sharpness leaving her speechless.

Realising she had overstayed her welcome, Liz left The Sea Platter, avoiding Christopher's gaze as she went. Her hopes of untying Paddy and hurrying back to her flat were dashed when Christopher slipped out of the restaurant after her.

"How are you feeling, Elizabeth?" Christopher asked, his brows dropping down at the sides while a smirk lingered behind faux sadness. "I heard about Simon's blast from the past coming back to town. I suppose that's put a dampener on your romance?"

Christopher reached out to rest a hand on Liz's shoulder, but she doubled back, avoiding his touch. Did he really think they were suddenly going to become an item because his competition was no longer in the picture? She thought back to their date again; they were painfully incompatible.

"I have to go," she said quickly as she wrapped Paddy's lead around her hand. "See you later."

She hurried down the street, not turning back to see if Christopher was watching her, even though she could feel his eyes burning into her back. She rounded the corner, letting out a frustrated sigh. Simon's face pushed forward in her mind, but she forced it back, not wanting to acknowledge her own disappointment.

"You didn't even kiss him," she reminded herself as she slotted the key into the flat door next to her shop, ready to go upstairs and paint the night away.

Five

E arly the next morning, Liz flipped her shop's sign from '*CLOSED*' to '*OPEN*'. She unlocked the door, wishing she could do nothing more than go back to bed with Paddy, but as things currently stood with the shop, she knew she had no option but to open. It was not that sales were bad, but they could have been better.

Standing on the doorstep, she inhaled the cool

morning air, its freshness waking her up in an instant. She looked towards the town square where the stallholders were setting up for the day. When she spotted Simon setting up his homemade cheese and ice cream stall, she took a step back into the comfort of the shop as she wrapped her thick cardigan protectively around her shoulders.

She watched him silently for a moment as he unloaded giant blocks of cheese onto his stall. Ellie, his little sister, was helping him arrange the display. She was so wrapped up in her scarf and hat, she was nothing more than a tiny pale face with golden pigtails poking out of the sides.

Liz smiled to herself, and for a moment, pretended everything was back to normal. As she watched Simon work, she could almost pretend they were back in that awkward place of talking about the weather and work without the obvious elephant in the room between them. As though she knew Liz was thinking about her, Natasha popped up from behind the stall, her dark hair curled beautifully away from her fresh face. Liz took another step back, scratching at the bun on her head, which currently held together with two old paintbrushes.

She turned to head back to the counter, but an amber leaf caught her attention as it drifted down from one of the trees dotted along the edge of the road. She watched its soft descent to the ground, the gentle morning breeze swirling it in the air. It landed in the middle of the road, its beauty maintaining her attention for an impossibly long time. It was technically dead, nothing more than a husk of its former self, but its beauty was at its peak; she wanted to paint it. Her attention was only broken when a car sped down the road, crunching the leaf into dust under its heavy tyre.

"*Liz!*" a tiny voice cried, dragging Liz's attention back to the market as she once again tried to head back into the safety of her shop.

With her pigtails fluttering in the wind, Ellie ran across the road, her fresh skin pink in the cold November air. Liz pushed forward a smile as she pulled her cardigan tighter across her body.

"Hello, Ellie," Liz said softly. "How's things?"

"I'm helping Simon on the stall today!" she exclaimed, her youthful excitement almost contagious. "He said I could have all the ice cream I wanted if I worked hard."

Liz looked back at the stall, her heart tightening when she saw Simon and Natasha looking in her direction. Liz widened her smile, hoping they could not see her discomfort from across the road.

"What's your favourite flavour?" Liz asked, turning her attention back to Ellie as she kicked up a cloud of dead leaves. "I like the vanilla."

"Chocolate with sprinkles," Ellie announced. "The leaves are the same colour as your hair. They're so pretty."

"They are," Liz agreed, bending down to pick one up. "Do you think I should have a go at painting one?"

Ellie nodded enthusiastically as she rubbed her runny nose with the back of her mitten. Liz carefully pocketed the leaf in the baggy pocket of her cardigan, knowing the shop would probably be quiet enough to spend the afternoon painting; it might even help her encourage some of her customers to buy paint.

Liz looked at the market again, her attention spiking when she saw Natasha resting a hand on Simon's shoulder. They looked as though they were disagreeing about something, making Liz wish she had supersonic hearing. Simon pulled away and continued to unbox the cheese, but Natasha set off towards Liz and Ellie. Panic surged through her as she wondered if she could feasibly retreat into the shop without having to face the woman, who was no less beautiful without her wedding dress, but when Natasha's eyes met Liz's, she knew she had to face her.

"Why don't you come to the farm anymore?" Ellie asked as she swung around a tree. "I miss you."

"Oh," Liz said, her voice shaking as Natasha grew closer. "I – erm –"

Natasha looked both ways before crossing the road, her feet seeming to slow down, as though she were approaching a dangerous animal. She was the complete opposite to Liz in every way possible. Without the disguise of the wedding dress and mascara streaks, Liz was able to look at her properly, and she was even more beautiful than she remembered. She was short in height in comparison to Liz's tall frame. She was also extremely tanned with thick, sleek dark hair. She wore a figure-hugging knee length dress with a leather jacket, and stylish boots with silver heels. Liz felt an unusual pang of jealousy.

"Ellie, you shouldn't run across the road without looking," Natasha said, her voice soft. "You always need to look."

"I know," Ellie said with a shrug as she sniffed. "I just wanted to come and see Liz."

Natasha threaded her hand around Ellie's as she turned her attention to Liz. Liz attempted to smile, but she was sure her lips were doing their best to snarl at the woman.

"I know you," Natasha said, her surprise unconvincing as she pointed a lazy finger at Liz. "You were at the farm."

A dry lump rose up in Liz's throat. She attempted to nod, but she felt like every muscle in her body had stiffened to stone.

"Yes," was all she could muster.

"Elizabeth, right?" she said with a curious smile. "Simon mentioned you."

"I prefer Liz," she replied bluntly. "I should really get back to my shop."

"Of course," Natasha said, her smile growing even more curious. "Simon's a great guy," she blurted out. "I don't know what I would do without him."

Natasha tossed her curls over her shoulder, wafting her sickly-sweet perfume in Liz's direction. It reminded her of Misty's dressing room.

"Simon *is* a good guy," Liz found herself saying with an agreeing nod. "I should really get back."

"Sure," Natasha said, turning to the road, only to turn back to Liz, her perfect brows furrowed slightly. "It's funny that Simon never mentioned you before, considering how good a friend you seem to be. We've always kept in touch."

"I'm new to town," Liz said, her voice scraping against her dry throat.

"Right," Natasha said with a nod as she turned back once more to the road. "It was nice to meet you properly, Elizabeth."

With Ellie in hand, Natasha headed back to the stall. Liz found her eyes fixed on the pair, only able to look away when Natasha touched Simon's arm again. She doubled back into the shop, slamming the door behind her. Eyes closed, she leaned her head against the cold glass. She knew exactly what Natasha had been trying to do, and she was frustrated that it had worked.

***

IN THE HOURS SINCE HER AWKWARD meeting with Natasha, Liz's shop had been busy, but she had hardly put anything through the till. The people of Scarlet Cove seemed more than happy to browse if it meant they could question Liz about her discovery at the castle. She felt like a fool for not even noticing that people were leaving empty handed until it happened for a third time. One woman had grabbed a bundle of wool after Liz pointed out that she was in a shop, and not a gallery after the woman had asked a dozen questions about Nathan.

A little after noon, Liz found herself flicking through her sketchpad. On her days off she would take her pad and pencil out into the town and scribble down things she might want to paint, but since Halloween she had been using her sketchpad for something else entirely.

She flicked to the page of notes, which had started out as a simple diagram of three names, but was now filled with her tiny scribbly handwriting.

Despite her mass of notes, she was no closer to figuring out why Nathan had been beheaded.

Tracing her finger along the three names she had circled, she landed on Polly Spragg. The quirky hairdresser certainly had a motive. Nathan had been cheating on her, and by her own admission, she had uncovered the affair right before the beheading. She also had the cut on her hand, which she said was from her hairdressing scissors. Could it have been from the murder weapon?

She traced her finger to the other side of the page, landing on Misty Rivers. Liz had written 'UNLIKEABLE' in big letters, which she had underlined three times. Just like Polly, she also had a solid motive. Had she killed Nathan because their affair had soured? The singer had seemed indifferent about her feelings towards Nathan, but had that been a cover? Liz had met liars just as convincing in her time in the force.

The final suspect she had was Daniel Clark, but the restaurant owner's notes were less extensive. She had nothing concrete, other than that Daniel had admitted he could not afford Nathan. She knew it was hardly a concrete motive for murder, but she had written his name down thanks to a feeling; her years of police work had taught her that a hunch could be better than hours in the forensics lab.

She pulled her phone from under her desk and scrolled to Miles' number. Glancing at the clock, she imagined him up in Manchester, tucking into one of his favourite falafel wraps on his lunch break while he worked on a case. He was the only person whom she had stayed in touch with after leaving the city, and she knew he might be able to provide an outsider's unbiased perspective. Hovering over the green icon, she prepared herself for the '*I told you that you wouldn't be able to stop poking your nose into murder*' speech.

She pressed the button, but the bell above the door decided her fate for her. She quickly ended the call after the first ring, tossing her phone onto the counter. She looked up with her friendliest customer service smile, but it faded when she saw Christopher striding into the shop, his hands in his suit trouser pockets as he looked around the place.

"Christopher," she said as she snapped the sketchpad shut. "What a nice surprise. After some paints?"

Christopher smiled politely as he approached the counter, his eyes drifting to the specially commissioned painting he had given to Liz to celebrate her shop's opening. She often looked at the picture to remind herself that Christopher Monroe was a real person and not just a ruthless business tycoon who had a tendency to look down his nose at people.

"I was just passing," he said as he stared down at the sketchpad. "Did I interrupt something?"

"Not at all," she said quickly, her cheeks burning. "I was just sketching."

Christopher smiled tightly at her. She did not know why he was there, but she could tell he had not been passing. She could not remember an instance since her shop's grand opening that Christopher had stepped foot inside.

"How's business?" he asked, looking around the empty shop with tight eyes. "Looks quiet."

"Booming as ever," Liz lied, unsure of why she did not want Christopher to know she was just about paying the bills on the place. "I'm the idiot who opened an arts and crafts shop at the end of a summer season, but I'm getting by."

"You are?" Christopher queried as he ran his finger along the counter. "Empty shelves?"

He cast a finger over to the wall of oil paints, where a good quarter of the paints were yet to be restocked.

"My supplier is squeezing every last penny out of me," she admitted, knowing that Christopher's business savvy persona would see through any lie she told. "It turned out that the good prices at the beginning were 'introductory offers', which had expiration dates. I never was good at paperwork."

"I have some contacts," he said with a pearly smile, baring his square perfect teeth like a shark about to eat its first meal of the day. "I could make some calls and see if I can find you someone cheaper."

"You would do that?"

"It's nothing," he said with a shrug. "Business is a game of knowing when to move and when to stick. I'm sure I can come up with someone willing to beat your current prices."

"That would actually be great," Liz said, almost under her breath. "I would really appreciate that."

"I'm always willing to help those in need,"

Christopher said with another casual shrug. "Especially those I like."

Liz gritted her teeth behind her smile as she clung to the counter. She hoped Christopher knew that her acceptance of his help would not lead to another awkward date and failed attempt at a kiss.

"Heard from Simon?" Christopher asked as he rubbed invisible dust between his fingers. "I thought I saw Natasha at the market with him earlier."

"It's none of my business."

"I'm sure it must have upset you?" he asked, his eyes darting up to meet hers, a pleased smile on his lips. "You *were* getting rather serious, or so I *heard*. It can't be easy to know that he ran back to his first love the second she turned up on his doorstep."

Liz considered showing Christopher where the door was, and she might have done if she had not caught a glimpse of the empty shelves out of the corner of her eye.

"Was there anything else?" she asked firmly. "I was just about to go through my inventory."

Christopher arched one of his faint brows, letting her know he knew he had pushed a button. Had that been his intention all along? Was he rubbing salt in the wound after she rejected him in favour of the farmer?

"I was just passing," he said again. "I'll make those calls when I get back to the office."

"Thank you."

Soft rain began to fall at the very moment Christopher walked towards the door. He ducked out of the shop and walked up the street. Liz heard a door slam and the roar of an engine starting up.

"Just passing, huh?" she grumbled to Paddy, who was curled up under the counter. "Who does he think he's fooling?"

The second she opened her sketchpad, the door opened again. She looked up excitedly, hoping to see an unfamiliar face who might want to buy some paints or PVA glue. She tried to hide her disappointment that it was just her landlord, Bob Slinger.

Bob shuffled into the shop in a yellow vinyl raincoat. The man was so small, the edge of the coat almost grazed the floor, only stopping a single inch above the rubber soles of his shoes. He sniffed, his bulbous nose redder than usual.

"I sensed rain," he said with a knowing nod as

he closed the door behind him. "You can never be too prepared."

"Looks like you were right," Liz said as rain began to bounce off the pavement. "How can I help you, Bob?"

"I got your message about the faulty boiler," he said with a wide smile, his eyes magnified to triple their size behind his spectacles. "It's been on the blink for years. I thought I'd take a look at it myself before I sent a man round. You never know, I might have the magic touch!"

He rubbed his hands together and shook them by his sides like a circus performer. Liz had always found her little landlord peculiar, but she liked him all the same. His unfaltering enthusiasm always perked her mood up a little.

"You know where it is," she said as she handed over her flat keys. "I think it's a problem with the timer."

Bob nodded as he pocketed the keys. He looked as though he was about to turn and get to work checking over the boiler, but he stopped, his finger rising up to his chin as though he had just remembered something.

"Nasty business with Nathan," he said, rocking steadily back and forth on his heels. "I read about it in the paper, although I heard about your involvement from Shirley at the Fish and Anchor."

"Word travels fast around here," Liz replied. "It seems that everyone in town knows me as the woman who kicked Nathan's head down a corridor."

"And it wasn't that long ago that you were the woman who uncovered the truth behind Frank's murder," he reminded her with a wag of his finger. "And I daresay it will be something entirely new next month. It's the way Scarlet Cove works. We have long memories, but fickle attention spans."

Liz wondered if that was possibly the wisest thing she had heard anyone say since arriving in Scarlet Cove. She looked the little man up and down, suddenly realising he probably knew more about the town than most.

"How long have you lived in Scarlet Cove, Bob?"

"Born and bred," he announced with a proud pat of his round stomach. "And the only time I'll be leaving is when it's in a box."

"Would you say you know what goes on around

this town?"

"Nothing gets past ol' Bob Slinger," he asserted with a tap on the side of his nose. "Tell me what you want to know?"

Liz mentally flicked through the notes she had, trying to locate the biggest gaps in her information.

"How well do you know Misty?"

"Misty Rivers?" he replied quickly, giving her hope that he would be a good source of information. "She's a bit of a loose cannon from what I've heard. Came into town like a whirlwind a couple of years ago. Started working at the cabaret bar when she took Derrick on as her talent agent."

"Derrick?" Liz responded, thinking back to the man she had seen rescuing Misty from Polly's attack during the Halloween party. "He didn't look like a talent agent."

"And I don't look like a landlord," he exclaimed jollily. "It's not his only job, but it's one of them. He does right by Misty, from what I know. He's going to make her a star."

Liz desperately wanted to open her sketchpad and scribble down everything he was saying, just in case something would be useful later on; she resisted.

"Do you know if Misty is working tonight?" Liz asked, knowing Coastline Cabaret's performance schedule might be a push for the old man to know. "I thought she was a great singer. I'd like to hear her again."

"I think she is," he said with a nod as his finger drummed against his chin. "In fact, I'm sure of it, and if she's not, you can have your next month's rent for free! She's always on the day after bingo, and I won five pounds last night."

Their conversation turned back to the weather before quickly tailing off. When he sensed his cue to leave, Bob pulled Liz's flat keys from his pocket, left the shop, and opened the door directly next to it.

With Bob banging and rattling around upstairs, Liz pulled out her phone. She had a missed call from Miles, along with a text message that read: '*Did you call me? Who's died now, Frizzy Lizzy?*'

Liz decided she would ring Miles later on for a proper catch-up, but she had someone else to call in the meantime. She scrolled to her second most called contact and pressed the phone against her ear.

"It's me," she said when Nancy picked up on the third ring. "Are you busy tonight?"

"I don't think so."

"Good. Fancy a trip to the cabaret bar?"

Six

Liz arrived at Coastline Cabaret ten minutes
before seven in the evening. It had always been
a habit of hers to arrive everywhere early, even
if no one else ever seemed to return the courtesy. She
stood in the doorway to fend off the cold, stepping
awkwardly to the side whenever people wanted to
enter.

Liz was relieved to hear Nancy's loud voice float along the wind a little after seven, but that relief quickly vanished when she saw who she was with. She had expected Nancy to bring Jack along, and had almost expected Nancy to forcibly drag Simon along, but she had not expected to see Natasha trailing behind.

"Sorry we're late," Nancy said, her eyes wide, apologising for more than just being late. "Let's get a drink."

Liz opened the door for Nancy but found herself glued into position. Jack walked through with his usual happy-go-lucky smile, and Simon followed with an awkward smile, his familiar musky aftershave tickling her nostrils. Natasha drifted through in a cloud of sickly-sweet perfume, her red-stained smile similar to the one she had given Liz outside her shop. Liz did not even try to return it.

"Bar," Nancy said, hooking her arm through Liz's and dragging her across the room. "Now."

Liz let herself be dragged through the half-empty bar. Nancy did not stop until they were at the bar and well out of earshot of Jack, Simon, and Natasha as they seated themselves at a table on the other side of the room.

"I asked Simon *specifically* not to bring her," Nancy said, her tone angry. "She tagged along anyway. Simon called Jack in a panic and didn't know how to tell her to stay at the farm."

"It's fine," Liz said, glancing back at the table, her stomach turning when she saw Natasha laughing at something, her hand resting on Simon's shoulder. "Honestly, I'm fine."

"I just wanted to get you in a room together *without* her," Nancy said as she dumped her handbag on the bar. "It's not fair. She's like a bad smell. I went up to the farmhouse to ask Simon what was happening, and she was stuck to him like Velcro. Even when I call, I can hear her in the background. I wouldn't be surprised if she sits by the door while he showers."

"What's there to talk about?" Liz said, hoping to catch Patsy's attention so she could change the subject. "It's none of my business."

Liz was beginning to feel like a broken record. It was not any of her business, but it felt like it should be. She looked back at Simon, surprised when she caught his eyes. He smiled across the room at her, but Liz whipped her head back to Nancy, unable to maintain eye contact.

"Twice in one week," Patsy exclaimed as she walked towards them in a tight, bright pink leopard-print top. "I'm a lucky woman. What can I get you girls?"

"Two wines, one orange juice, and two beers please," Nancy said as she plucked her purse from her bag.

"*Orange juice?*" Patsy asked. "Not drinking tonight?"

"It's for *Natasha*," Nancy choked out, the word sticking in her throat like it did Liz's. "She's back, and apparently doesn't like wine anymore."

"Simon's ex-girlfriend?" Patsy asked, her brows arching up her taut forehead. "What's she doing back in Scarlet Cove? I thought she swanned off to be a lawyer?"

"She's a lawyer?" Liz asked disbelievingly. "My parents would love her. Maybe I should call them and ask if they want a new daughter?"

"She's got nothing on you," Patsy said with a wink as she poured the wine. "This one is for you, Liz. You look like you need it."

Patsy handed Liz a glass full to the rim. She was more than grateful when the alcohol hit her lips.

They headed back to the table, but Liz found her attention turning to the corridor where she knew Misty's dressing room was. She placed Jack's beer in front of him, avoiding Simon and Natasha's obvious gazes.

"I'll be right back," she said, already wandering off with the glass of wine in her hands.

She lingered by the entrance of the corridor for a moment. The bar was moderately busy, but nothing like it had been on Halloween. Just as Nancy had warned, it was mainly filled with the older residents along with unsuspecting tourists.

"*Derrick?*" Misty's voice echoed down the corridor. "Derrick? Are you there?"

Liz hung back for a moment, waiting for the balding man to appear. When he did not, she slipped down the corridor and into Misty's dressing room.

"Oh," Misty said when she caught Liz's eyes in the mirror. "You again. Where's Derrick?"

"He's coming," Liz lied, looking around the extravagantly decorated room that she had not had a chance to look at during her first interaction with Misty. "He told me to tell you he's been held up."

Excessive garments and leotards sparkled from long racks, sequins and jewels catching the soft light of Misty's dressing table mirror. Giant headpieces sat on plastic heads along the far wall, with heavy-looking costume jewellery hanging on hooks underneath them. Amongst all the excess Liz felt like a magpie unable to focus on one shiny thing at a time.

"They're quite something, aren't they?" Misty smiled in the mirror as she applied some loose powder across the bridge of her nose.

"They're beautiful." Liz walked over to the rack, her fingers dancing across the different fabrics. "Have you ever thought about performing in Vegas?"

"I have bigger dreams than Vegas," Misty said, her smile smug in the warm glow of the bulbs. "That's not all of it. I have more in storage, although I'm sure things keep going missing."

"You wear all of this here?" Liz asked.

"No way," she scoffed as she ran a tiny comb through her neat brows. "They were too expensive. I wouldn't waste them here. I'm destined for greater things than this tiny town."

Liz turned away from the costumes. She joined Misty in the mirror and watched as she expertly finished her makeup. There was no denying her beauty. Her pale powdered skin looked soft to the touch, her lips naturally plump and luscious. She reminded Liz of a silent movie star, and she considered that she might like the entertainer a lot more if she did not have the ability to voice her arrogance.

"This town isn't so bad," Liz said with a shrug as her eyes danced over the twenty or so makeup brushes, none of which she knew the use for. "I love it here."

"It's okay for *some* people," Misty said, her eyes darting up and down Liz's simple exterior in a flash. "Derrick is going to help me get out of here. He has a brother who works in the West End in London. Scouts are going to be coming any day, and then I'll be on a first-class ticket out of here. First the West End, and then Hollywood."

"Won't you miss Scarlet Cove?" Liz asked as she watched Misty apply blood-red lipstick. "It has beautiful views."

"It's a dump," she said, her lips barely moving as she finished lining her pout. "Some places deserve fish and chips, and some places deserve caviar. I'm caviar, and I deserve a better platter to showcase my worth."

The door to the dressing room opened, and the balding man with the glasses who had parted Polly and Misty walked in.

"Be humble, my star," he said, glancing sceptically at Liz as he strode to Misty's side. "It's only a matter of time before my brother sends his talent scouts, and then you can live the life you're destined for. Beautiful, talented women like you shouldn't flounder in places like this."

Misty beamed at Derrick in the mirror as he rubbed her shoulders. Liz wondered what had come first; Misty's ego or Derrick's smoke blowing.

"I hope your brother gets here sooner rather than later," Misty said, exhaling heavily before applying blush to her pale cheeks. "This place is sucking out my energy. I need a bigger stage."

"And you'll get it," Derrick assured her. "But you have to pay your dues. My brother is busy, but he's given me his word that he will be here the second he can tear himself away. Your future is as good as secured if you stick with me, but until then, you have an audience waiting."

Liz took that as her cue to leave, not that she could stand another second of Derrick's ego-inflating pep talk. She left them alone in the dressing room, sipping her wine as she headed back to the table. When she saw Natasha hanging off Simon's every word, she wanted to head straight for the door, but she knew it would send the wrong message.

"Where did you go?" Nancy asked as Liz sat next to her, glad she was on the opposite side of the table from Natasha and Simon. "Bathroom?"

"Something like that."

While they waited for Misty's performance to begin, Jack and Nancy chatted about work, leaving Liz to sit and stare at Natasha and Simon, who seemed to be in a world of their own. They spoke in low whispers, Natasha's giggles breaking the silence every minute or so. She caught Simon looking up at her more than once, but when she sensed his eyes on her, she made sure to stare patiently at the stage.

When the lights finally dimmed, the applause

started. Liz was glad of the distraction, even if she could still hear Natasha's shrill giggles over the roar of the crowd.

The red velvet curtains parted, and Misty took centre stage. She looked every inch the starlet in a gold floor-length sparkling gown. The backing track for The Pointer Sisters' '*Fire*' started, and she began to sway and sing. After hearing Misty talk in the dressing room, Liz had expected an excellent voice to leave the woman's lips, so she was surprised when she heard a soft, almost baby-like sound echo around the bar. Without the backing dancers and costumes to act as a distraction, she was just an average singer in a pretty dress.

Liz looked around the bar. The elderly folks were tapping their feet, and the tourists were watching with interest, but the half-empty bar was very different from the raving audience Derrick talked about. Liz spotted Derrick in the wings of the stage. He shot Misty a thumbs up, not that she could see him. Liz picked up her wine, her eyes landing on Natasha and Simon. In the dark, she felt safer watching them without being seen. Natasha looked at Simon the same way Nancy looked at Jack, and even though he was not returning the look, he was also not pulling away from her hand, which was resting on his shoulder.

Liz polished off her wine, told Nancy she needed the bathroom, and headed straight for the door. As she walked home in the dark, the bitter cold biting at her skin, she managed to think of forty-three other things she would rather do than sit in a cabaret bar with Simon and Natasha.

Seven

It had become part of Liz's routine to walk down to the seafront with Paddy after closing the shop. She had thought the routine would stop when the weather turned, but she had found a comfort in wrapping up warmly and walking against the bitter wind. It reminded her she was alive, and her brain was never more active than when she was inhaling the icy sea air.

With Paddy pulling on her arm, she walked past Coastline Cabaret. It was still early in the evening, but it seemed busy inside. She heard someone call *'eighty-eight! It's two fat ladies'* followed by a woman shrieking *'BINGO'*. She wondered how Misty spent her days off. She could not imagine her sitting at home with her feet up watching television like the rest of the town.

She reached the harbour, her mind firmly on Nathan. It felt like most of Scarlet Cove had already forgotten about the beheading, as though it was now just an extension of the ghost story, which would stay buried until next Halloween. She had been checking the local paper's website for updates, but the police did not seem any closer to figuring things out than she was. It was not that she wanted to get there first; she just wanted a resolution.

She reached the harbour and noticed Christopher's office lights were on. She walked down the jetty towards the warm glow, glad when she saw Christopher working behind his desk.

"Elizabeth," Christopher said with a smile, jumping up and opening the door. "What a pleasant surprise. How can I help you?"

"I was wondering if you had made any of those calls yet?" she asked, the growing emptiness of her shelves burning a hole in the back of her mind. "For the suppliers?"

"Ah, yes," he said with a nod, pulling the door open. "Come in."

She walked into the tiny office followed by Paddy. The heat from a portable gas fire was so intense, it took her a second to catch her breath. After unravelling her scarf, she sat on the other side of the desk, and Paddy curled up by her feet.

Christopher shuffled through a stack of papers, his brow creased. For a brief moment, she wondered if his promise of finding a supplier had been bravado on his part. She was a little surprised when he withdrew a sheet of paper with a green sticky note labelled '*Elizabeth Jones*' attached to the top.

"Here they are," he said, handing them across the table. "I'll make some coffee while you have a look through the numbers."

The last time she had been in Christopher's office, she had been trying to find clues linked to the murder of his head fisherman, Frank. Christopher had been one of her suspects for a brief moment, and even though the fatal rat poison that had led to the man's demise had belonged to Christopher, he had had nothing to do with the murder; she was happy to see the rat poison was gone.

She scanned the paperwork, relieved to see that most of her favourite brands were there, and even more pleased to see the huge difference in price from what she was currently paying.

"I can't believe how cheap this is," she said, looking at him sceptically. "Is there a catch?"

Christopher handed over a coffee, his tight smile giving away that he seemed a little offended at the suggestion that he would try to trick her.

"There's no catch," he said as he resumed his seat. "I give you my word."

Liz looked over the prices again. When she had first started looking at suppliers to stock her shop, she had hit a brick wall more than once. All the places with the good prices had wanted her to make huge quantity minimum orders, which was what had led her to her current supplier. Now that they had her up against a wall, she wondered if they had seen her coming a mile off.

"This will really help," Liz said as she folded up

the paper. "Thank you so much."

Liz stuck around and finished her coffee. To her surprise, Christopher did not try to inject Simon into the conversation, nor did he suggest that they go on another date. Instead, they chatted idly about the weather and local gossip; it made a pleasant change.

When Liz left Christopher's office, she intended to go straight home to spend some quality time with a bottle of wine, but instead she felt compelled to walk past Crazy Waves after one of Christopher's gossip titbits had revealed that Polly was apparently back at work. When she saw the young stylist sitting behind a desk in the empty salon, Liz tied Paddy to a lamppost, unable to walk by without checking how she was.

She walked up the two steps to the salon door and pushed it open, the electric shop bell chiming out. Polly jumped up from her position behind the nail desk where she had been absently filing her nails.

"Liz?" she asked, squinting into the dark. "Are you here for a trim?"

Liz glanced at the clock on the wall. It was

almost six in the evening, and she was sure that Polly's salon closed at five, just like her own shop. Despite this, the hope in Polly's eyes told Liz she should probably accept the offer; her hair did need a trim.

"If it's not too late?" Liz asked. "Can I bring Paddy in?"

"Sure," Polly said as she reached for her scissors. "It's not like anyone else is here."

Liz untied Paddy and brought him into the shop. He immediately jumped up onto one of the bright red leather stylist chairs, his tongue lolling out the side of his mouth. Liz knew he would stay there until she was ready to leave.

She sat in her usual middle chair and unravelled her scarf. Polly wrapped a gown around her neck, her smile subdued in the mirror. She no longer had red, puffy eyes, her usual beehive was a simple, neat ponytail, and she had applied a little makeup, but she still looked nothing like the usually tanned and preened Essex girl Liz had grown used to.

"How are you?" Liz asked as Polly gently combed through Liz's bushy, knotted hair. "You look well."

"I'm just taking it day by day," she said with a shrug. "I thought coming back to work would make me feel better, but it hasn't. I haven't had a single customer all day. I called all my regulars this morning to let them know I was back. They all offered sympathies and all that rubbish, but nobody booked an appointment."

"They probably don't know what to say," Liz offered. "They'll come back. You're good at your job."

Polly paused her combing for a moment and rested her hand on her chest. She looked as though she might cry, but she held it together. She grabbed her scissors and started on Liz's split ends.

"I thought you'd be closed by now," Liz offered as she glanced at the clock in the mirror. "I was passing on the off-chance and saw the lights."

"I can't stand being cooped up in that house any longer," Polly admitted, her lips curling up at the edges. "I still have all of Nathan's things. I can't bring myself to sort it out, but I can't bear looking at it for another day."

"I've been there," Liz said, remembering how difficult it had been to sort through Lewis' shirts and records. "In my experience, the sooner you start, the better you'll feel."

Polly did not say anything, instead choosing to simply nod. She seemed to get lost in the cutting, so Liz decided against interrupting. She did not care about her looks as much as most women, but the last thing she wanted was a wonky cut. When Polly was finished, she ran some product through Liz's frizzy hair before pulling off the gown.

"I miss him," Polly said, her eyes wide and blank as she clung to the gown. "I should hate him, and a part of me does, but I still miss him."

She could not hold her tears back this time, so Liz reached into her handbag for a packet of tissues.

"Thank you," Polly said, pulling one out to blow her nose. "It's not normal, is it? He cheated on me, and he was using me, but I still loved him. My love was real, even if his wasn't. How do I get over that, Liz?"

Liz wished she had the answers. She thought about what had happened with Simon, and a hard lump formed in her throat. Did she love Simon? She was not sure if she wanted to answer that.

"If you need any help with Nathan's things, I

could help?" Liz offered, deciding it was better to be proactive than just offer empty words of sympathy. "I know it's none of my business, but –,"

"Are you sure?" Polly jumped in, her eyes lighting up. "I wouldn't want to ruin any plans you might have."

"I don't have any plans," Liz said. "Well, I was going to start on a bottle of wine, but I can bring that with me. I could ask Nancy to help? We'll get it done in no time with the three of us."

Polly nodded as a soft smile pricked up her lips. It warmed Liz to know that she might have made a tiny difference in Polly's day. She thought back to her darkest days after Lewis' death, and it had been the kindness of strangers that had got her through. Strangers holding open a door, or letting her jump the line at the supermarket because she was only buying a carton of milk had lifted her days. Flowers and sympathy cards from friends had made little difference.

"Why are you being so nice to me?" Polly asked as Liz plucked money from her purse. "Everyone else is avoiding me like the plague."

"I know how you feel," Liz said as she handed

over the money, which included a generous tip. "Everyone deserves a bit of kindness, and I like you, Polly."

Leaving Polly to close up the salon, Liz headed home to drop Paddy back at the flat with a promise to return quickly. She walked across the empty market square, horror rising up within her when she spotted Simon and Natasha heading into Driftwood Café with Ellie in between them, each holding one of her hands.

Liz did not know what possessed her, but she quickly crouched behind a bin. She glanced over it, relieved when she saw them inside the café. She thought she might have got away with her embarrassing move, but then she saw Misty marching across the square, a phone clutched against her ear.

The singer stopped in her tracks to stare down at Liz like she was a piece of dirt on her shoe. Liz smiled clumsily at Misty, who looked as beautiful as always, even though she was only wearing jeans and a cream double-breasted trench coat.

"What on Earth are you doing?" she asked, holding her phone against her shoulder. "You look crazy."

"I dropped something."

Misty seemed to decide against giving Liz any more of her time. She pushed her phone back up against her ear and continued her marching.

"Derrick, you *need* to get me out of this place. It's *full* of *freaks*."

Liz stood up as she listened to Misty's stiletto heels clicking on the cobbles. She looked in the direction of Driftwood Café, not surprised to see Simon and Natasha looking in her direction. Ellie waved, so Liz waved back, but she avoided looking at Simon and Natasha as she hurried to her flat door.

Eight

"It's very *pink*," Nancy said as she stepped into Polly's sitting room. "It's very you, Polly."

Liz shot Nancy a look to tell her to play nice, but she shrugged as though she did not know what she had done wrong.

"Thanks," Polly said as she followed them in, still in her clothes from the salon. "Try and ignore the mess if you can. I haven't really felt up to cleaning."

Liz looked around the small living room, and it became painfully obvious that Polly had not tidied since her last visit. The pizza boxes were stacked even higher, and there were now wine bottles to match.

"Who wants wine?" Nancy announced jovially as she pulled two bottles from a blue plastic bag. "It's the good stuff."

Polly nodded awkwardly, her cheeks blushing as she looked around her messy living room. Liz smiled at her to let her know it was okay. Liz's home had looked similar after her own loss.

"I couldn't find any clean glasses, so I suppose mugs will have to do," Nancy announced after rummaging through the kitchen. "They're big mugs though, so it means less pouring."

Nancy poured the first bottle into the three mugs, only leaving a little behind in the bottom. Not seeming able to waste it, she emptied the rest of the bottle into her mouth as her first sip. Liz only took a small mouthful, deciding it would be better to work with a clear head.

"Right, ladies," Liz said, clapping her hands together. "Before we start on Nathan's stuff, why don't we get your house back to normal? I'll start in here. Nancy, you can do the washing up."

"Ugh," Nancy moaned with a pout. "I *hate* washing up. I always get Jack to do it."

Nancy shuffled reluctantly into the kitchen, leaving Liz and Polly in the living room. Liz flicked on a pink radio, which was tuned into a pop station. She grabbed the roll of black bags that she had brought from her flat and yanked off two of them. She passed one to Polly and shook open her own. It only took ten minutes for them to reclaim Polly's living room from the mess.

"That's better," Liz said after tying up the second bag. She planted her hands on her hips and looked around at their handiwork, glad they had already made a noticeable difference before they had even finished their first mug of wine. "Where's Nathan's stuff?"

"Most of it is still in the bedroom," Polly said, brushing stray strands of her hair away from her face. "I haven't really been sleeping there. I've been sleeping on the couch. I'm not sure if I'm ready to do this."

"I'll sort the bedroom," Liz said, planting a hand

firmly on Polly's shoulder. "Stay down here with Nancy and gather up anything that needs to go."

After a big mouthful of wine, Polly nodded her agreement. She ripped off another bag before squatting in front of the DVD collection under the television.

Liz tore off a couple of bags before heading up the narrow staircase to the landing, which had been decorated in the same pink and white zebra print paper as the chimney breast. Another miniature black chandelier hung from the low ceiling, its hanging jewels almost scraping the top of Liz's head. There were only three rooms. After looking in the bathroom, which was also bright pink, and a junk room, which had a Pilates machine buried under boxes of Christmas decorations and old clothes, she headed to the final door at the end of the short hall.

Just like the front room, Polly's bedroom was impossibly girly. Instead of the hot pink of the rest of the house, she had opted for a more subdued dusky pink. She stepped into the dark room and flicked on the ceiling light. The mirror-sequined lampshade glittered brightly over the walls.

The mixture of sweet perfume and aftershave hit

her immediately. Clothes were strewn across the room, making it obvious which side had been Nathan's.

Hoodies, shirts, and men's jeans littered one side of the room, while bras, frilly underwear, and dresses littered the other. Liz began by bagging up the dirty clothes, and after a quick inspection of the drawers, she found which belonged to Nathan. Like most men she had known, his collection of clothes was minimal, meaning she was done with them quicker than she expected. The radio turned up downstairs, and Polly's distinctive girlish giggle drifted up the stairs, warming Liz. She knew she could rely on Nancy to brighten almost any situation.

She moved to the aftershave bottles cluttered on his nightstand. She sniffed a couple, but they were all too strong for her tastes. She thought about the subtle musky fragrance Simon wore, which had an effect on her she could not explain. She wondered if she would ever get close enough to smell it again.

After emptying the bedside drawers without looking too closely at the contents, she moved onto a stack of books on the floor. The top book was coated with a silvery layer of dust, letting her know it had not been read in a while. She picked them up one at a time, pausing to scan over the blurbs. When it came to the last book, she instantly recognised it as Stephen King's *Carrie*, a book she had read in her youth after it had done the rounds at the school library.

She flicked through the book on its way to the black bag, but paused when a piece of paper fluttered out, landing by her shoe. She picked it up, assuming it had been used as a crude bookmark. Out of curiosity, she unfolded the piece of paper, surprised that it was a hand-written note scrawled over the top of a wage slip. She looked back at the bedroom door as more giggles drifted up from the sitting room.

For a brief moment, Liz considered tossing the piece of paper without reading it. A small part of her felt wrong for intruding on a dead man's privacy, but the detective within her was far too curious.

She looked over the letter and read the scribbly handwriting:

'You can't keep avoiding me. You better pay me what you owe me, or else. You know I can't afford to keep doing this. D.'

She turned the letter over, hoping to see more, but there was nothing.

"'*You better pay me what you owe me*'," Liz read aloud. "'*You know I can't afford to keep doing this*'."

Liz tossed the Stephen King book into the bag with the others, but she folded the paper and pushed it into the back pocket of her jeans. She knew it might be nothing, and it was far from concrete evidence, but if the letter was from who she thought, it was the best lead she had discovered since the murder.

The music began to vibrate the walls as the radio was cranked up even louder. After quickly folding up Polly's clothes and changing the bed sheets, she cracked open the window slightly to let some fresh air in before heading downstairs.

When Liz walked into the sitting room with the black bags, she was not surprised to see two empty mugs and a good chunk of the second bottle missing. Even though they were both sloppily pushing CDs into a bag, which had a giant hole in the bottom, Liz was glad to see Polly smiling again.

"We've had a great idea," Nancy exclaimed when she spotted Liz. "Haven't we, Polly?"

Polly pushed her finger against her lips and shushed, her eyes blinking as she forced back a giggle. Liz wondered if it had been such a good idea to leave Nancy and Polly alone after all.

"We should take all this stuff to Misty's house and dump it on her doorstep," Nancy said, grabbing the CD rack to drag herself up to her feet. "She wanted him, so she can have him."

"That is most definitely *not* a good idea." Liz cried, planting her hands on her hips. "How quickly did you drink that wine?"

Nancy helped Polly up to her feet, the two women suddenly appearing to be the best of friends.

"Misty will know it's a *joke*," Nancy said. "She's got a *great* sense of humour."

"That woman has *no* sense of humour," Polly added with a devious grin as she poured more wine into her mug. "It's the *perfect* idea."

Liz did not want to seem like the old boring one, but she did not have wine or grief clouding her judgement. She picked up her untouched mug and took a sip, but it had been a while since she had been on Nancy and Polly's level, and she knew it would take more than a giant mug of wine to get there.

"Is that *his* stuff from my bedroom?" Polly said, swaying slightly as she cast a finger at the black bags by the door. "It's less than I thought."

"I think I got it all," Liz replied, the note burning a hole in her back pocket. "If there's anything else, I'll -"

Before Liz could say another word, Polly dived for the bags, almost toppling over as she picked them up.

"Careful," Liz said as she tried to steady Polly. "What have you two been drinking?"

"We *may* have done shots," Nancy said with a shrug as she stuffed more CDs into the bag. "Vodka and wine mix, right?"

Liz's stomach turned at the thought. She had not drunk so recklessly since her days studying fine art at university. Now that she understood why the women were so drunk, she knew there was nothing she could say to dissuade them.

Polly headed for the front door with the two bags from the bedroom, and Nancy followed with the bags from downstairs, not seeming to notice one was leaking CDs as she weaved past Liz.

"Maybe we should talk about this?" Liz called

after them as they hurried down the garden path. "It's late, and you've been drinking."

Liz had no idea where Misty lived, but Polly seemed to know exactly where she was going. She followed them along the twisting narrow streets as they headed further up the hill. She protested regularly, but she was ignored and met with more giggles.

Polly finally stopped in front of a small, detached house with a neat garden. From the outside, it looked modest, and nothing like the lavish home Misty likely wanted for herself, but it still looked like it cost more to rent than Liz's small flat.

"If you get caught I had *nothing* to do with this," Liz whispered as they crouched behind a bush at the bottom of the garden. "This is the worst possible idea."

Liz peered over the bush and looked through the front window. The blinds were open, and she spotted Misty walking towards a fridge in a silk negligée. She grabbed a bottle of wine from the fridge, unaware that she was being watched.

Still crouching, Polly unclipped the gate. It

swung open and creaked into the night, making Liz wince. She looked back to the front window to see if Misty had heard them, but she was pouring a glass of wine. Liz almost bobbed back down as Polly and Nancy crept along the garden path with the bags, but she spotted movement around the side of the cottage. She squinted into the dark, but she could not see anything. Leaving Polly and Nancy to continue on their journey to the front door, Liz crept to the edge of the bush. She stood up, just in time to see a dark figure running along the side of the house towards the back garden. Nancy and Polly started giggling at nothing, pulling her attention.

"Shush!" Liz flared at them, holding up a finger. "There's someone -"

As soon as she turned back, the figure had gone. Polly and Nancy dumped the bags on Misty's doorstep, giggling like naughty schoolchildren. They scurried back down the path towards Liz, who was still looking down the side of the house. Had she imagined it? She blinked hard, sure she had seen something. Before she could decide if she was going to check it out, she locked eyes with Misty through the blinds. Liz smiled apologetically as she let Nancy and Polly drag her back down.

"What have you got me into?" Liz hissed.

Nine

Liz looked out of her shop window as heavy rain pounded against the road. She had hoped she would not have another quiet day at work, but she could not imagine many people wanting to brave the rain for the sake of some paints.

Letting out a heavy sigh, she sipped some of her green tea before looking back at the stock list Christopher had given her. If things carried on like they were, it did not matter how cheap the she made her prices, she would not be able to stay open forever. She had poured every penny she had ever saved into starting her new life in Scarlet Cove, and part of that new life had been to open her arts and crafts business. She had expected the shop to be turning a small profit by now, but according to the latest spread sheets from her accountant, she was just about breaking even.

The bell above the door rang out, bringing with it the sound of the heavy rain. She shot up, excitement coursing through her, but that excitement quickly turned to dread when the new customer pulled down his hood to reveal that he was not a customer at all.

Simon closed the door behind him before shaking the water off his raincoat. He smiled hesitantly at her, something clutched in his hands.

"Simon?"

"Hi, Liz," he said uncomfortably as he rubbed the back of his neck with one hand while the other offered the small package. "I brought you some cheese."

She stared at the cheese for a moment, unsure

how to react. She met Simon's eyes, all of the familiar feelings flooding back. She gulped hard, remembering the Natasha shaped wedge between them. Unwilling to pretend a block of cheese would fix things, even if it was delicious, she looked back down at the paperwork; the words blurred together.

Simon hurried across the shop to place the cheese on the edge of the counter. He quickly darted back, as though he had just left her a stick of dynamite.

"Thank you," she said, forcing a cough as she shuffled through the papers. "No Natasha today?"

"She's at the farmhouse," he explained with a shrug as his red nose twitched. "She's baking with Mum."

"How lovely."

"You know she's just a friend, don't you?"

"She is?" Liz retorted. "Does *she* know that?"

Simon squinted at her as though he had no idea what Liz was trying to say. She laughed to herself, wondering if he could really be that naïve.

"I don't understand," Simon shot back. "I've known her for years. She's just in a spot of trouble right now, that's all."

"You don't need to explain yourself to me, Simon. It's your business what you do."

"But I feel like I need to explain," Simon said, taking a brave step forward. "I'm just trying to get her back on her feet."

Liz placed the papers on the counter. She wanted to believe him, but she had seen the way Natasha looked at him. Liz parted her lips, but she stopped herself when she quickly remembered how Simon had not been in touch since Natasha's sudden appearance at the farm. When it came down to it, actions spoke louder than words.

"Putting in a stock order?" Simon asked, out of the blue, as he looked down at the paperwork.

"I'm thinking about it," she replied. "Christopher gave me some details for a new company."

"C-Christopher?" he said, the words catching in his throat. "You're trusting *him*?"

"Yes, Christopher."

"Why are you letting him help?" Simon huffed. "I thought you didn't even like him?"

"Why are you helping Natasha?" she replied quickly. "It's the same thing."

"No, it isn't. It's completely different. He's trying to worm his way in."

"It's just work," she said as she quickly gathered up the papers. "It's not like I was ever in love with Christopher."

"I – I -"

"You're a good guy, Simon," Liz said after draining the rest of her green tea. "Natasha is lucky to have you."

Simon stared at her with wide eyes and flared nostrils. He looked as though he might burst into tears, or trash the shop; Liz hoped for neither.

"I think I should leave," he said quietly, dropping his head. "I'm sorry I came."

"Fine," she shot back.

"Fine," he echoed.

Simon did not immediately move, and Liz was not sure that she wanted him to. She hated how uncomfortable things were between them. Even if he was just helping Natasha as a friend, it did not explain why he had been giving Liz the cold shoulder for the past week.

When he did finally move, Liz was surprised that he took a step forward, and not back. He stared at her for a moment, his lips tight as his cheeks reddened. He looked as though he was going to say something, and her heart screamed out for him to, so she was more than a little hurt when he scooped up the cheese and headed for the door. He pulled his hood back over his head and stormed off into the rain.

"You stupid woman," she whispered under her breath as she beat her forehead against the counter. "*Stupid, stupid, stupid.*"

Liz had always known she was stubborn. As a child, she had sat at the dinner table for almost five hours because her father had told her she could not leave until she had eaten her broccoli. In the end, her mother had sent her up to her bed, and the broccoli had found its way into the bin. She knew it was never a good idea to get two stubborn people into the middle of a misunderstanding because neither would back down when they needed to.

Liz lifted her head off the counter just in time to see Daniel ducking into the shop. She was just as surprised to see him as she had been when Simon appeared.

"Nice weather we're having," Daniel said with a

shaky smile. "Do you sell chalk? I've been looking everywhere, and I can't seem to find any."

Liz walked around the counter, happy that she could help a real customer for once. She picked up a multipack of different coloured chalks before passing it to Daniel.

"You're a life saver," he said with a relieved laugh. "I wiped down the menu boards at The Sea Platter before I realised I didn't have anything to rewrite them with."

"Changing the menu?" she asked as she walked back to the counter.

"More like the prices," he admitted. "If things carry on like they are, I'll be out of business by the end of the week."

Liz swallowed the lump that rose in her throat. Was this the reality of owning a business in a seasonal tourist town? She punched the item into the till before bagging up the chalk. She handed it over to Daniel, who looked like he was already desperate to leave. She wondered if it had anything to do with their awkward interaction at the restaurant, and if he had been searching for chalk everywhere else so as not to have to face her.

"I was helping Polly get rid of Nathan's things last night," she said before Daniel turned to leave. "I found your note."

"W-what note?"

Liz reached into her back pocket when she realised she was wearing the same jeans as she had at Polly's. She read over the small hand-written note again before dropping it onto the counter. When all of the colour drained from the restaurant owner's face, she knew she was looking at 'D'.

"Would I be right in thinking you never got your money back before he died?" Liz asked as she sat on the stool behind the counter. "Forgive me if I'm being presumptuous."

"No," he mumbled, his brows drawing together. "No, I didn't. I know what you must think. I know you're a detective, and you're probably assuming -"

"*Ex*-detective," she corrected him. "And I'm not assuming anything. I could have taken this straight to the police, but I didn't."

"I *didn't* kill him," Daniel said quickly as he reached out for the note with shaky hands. "I only threatened him to rattle his cage. It was stupid. I'd had a couple of beers when I wrote the note. I was hoping it would push him to pay back the money I'd lent him. It was nine hundred pounds, which might not sound a lot, but it's the difference between me staying open or going bankrupt. Things were going well when I gave him the money. It was early summer, and the weather was good. You never think the good times are going to end, do you? He came to me on a day when I'd had record takings. He said he needed the money to fix his car, and I was the idiot who just handed it over. He said he'd pay me back by the end of the month, but he didn't. I even tried taking it out of his wages, but he kept saying he had nothing. I felt sorry for him. Things wouldn't be this bad if Fishy Chris didn't keep jacking his prices up."

"And now you're struggling because of it."

"When I found out he had two women on the go, I wasn't surprised," he said with a dark chuckle. "Must have been expensive keeping up, especially as far as Misty is concerned. Look, I need to go. I'm opening up in half an hour, and I haven't even started my prep."

"Wait," Liz said, jumping up, her hand outstretched. "What do you know about Misty?"

"Listen, I don't want to get involved," Daniel said, the chalk in one hand, his other on the door handle. "I went on a date with her when she first arrived in town. She's ignored my calls since. It wasn't meant to be. I just want to stay out of things."

Daniel scurried out of the shop and into the rain, leaving Liz hungry for more information. She looked down for the note, but Daniel had taken it with him.

"*Dammit!*" she cried, her fist striking the counter. Paddy jumped up from his slumber, one ear poking up. "Not you, boy. Go back to sleep."

Paddy curled back up in the corner of the shop, but darted straight back up again when the shop door slammed in its frame once more. A large black umbrella retracted to reveal Misty, completely dry.

"What do you think you're playing at?" she spat as she marched towards the counter, shaking her wet umbrella all over Liz's shop. "I saw you last night!"

"Excuse me?"

"Don't act like you don't know what I'm talking about!" Misty slapped her hands on the table, spraying Liz and her paperwork with rainwater.

"That bright, *frizzy* hair is a little hard to miss. Ever heard of conditioner?"

"First of all, I was only there to stop them from doing something stupid," Liz said, getting to her feet. "Second of all, I'm sorry. They were drunk."

"Who's '*they*'?" she exclaimed. "That bimbo, Polly, I guess? What on Earth am I supposed to do with all that stuff? And don't even get me started on those roses!"

"What roses?"

"No wonder you were a detective!" Misty shrieked, her pale cheeks flushing. "You're a good actress. Stop playing dumb."

"I really don't know what you mean," Liz said, folding her arms as she frowned at the singer. "What roses?"

Misty stared at Liz for a moment as though she was about to launch into a rant about how good a liar Liz was, but she seemed to notice something in Liz's eyes that made her stop. She deflated a little, her beautifully groomed brows curling sharply.

"Weird stuff has been happening recently," Misty started, her voice smaller and more fragile. "Someone shoved roses through my letter box, and my costumes have been going missing from my dressing room. I thought it might be you since you keep popping up *everywhere* all of a sudden."

"I swear on Paddy's life, I don't have anything to do with any of that," Liz said, holding her hands up. "Have you gone to the police?"

Misty shook her head as she glanced at Paddy in the corner. Her softened edges prickled back up, her eyes narrowing on Liz.

"I don't know why I'm telling *you* any of this," she snapped. "You're nobody."

Liz ignored Misty's insult because she was surer than ever that she had not been seeing things after all. She swallowed hard, wondering how to say it without scaring Misty.

"Did you have any guests last night?" Liz asked, taking her seat once more.

"Apart from you, no."

"Then I'm sorry to say this, but I saw someone looking through your window," Liz said, her voice calm as her police training took over. "I saw a figure dressed in black at the side of your house. I thought maybe I had imagined it, but after what you've just told me, it makes perfect sense."

"W-Who was it?"

"I don't know," Liz admitted. "I didn't get a proper look. I almost chased after them, but you saw me, and I panicked."

"You expect me to believe that?" Misty said, forcing an unsure laugh. "You're just trying to frighten me. You're jealous."

"I'm not lying," Liz said firmly. "What would I have to gain? I'm a painter, not a singer. I'm not a threat to you."

"Well, whatever," Misty said as she took a quick step back. "Just back off, okay? If you and that bimbo pull another stunt like last night, I'll call the police."

"Okay," Liz said with a nod. "Fair enough."

"I need to go," Misty announced as she pushed her umbrella back up. "The talent scouts from London are coming tonight, and you and your *frizziness* are messing up my energy."

She stormed out of the shop, leaving Liz and Paddy alone once again. They looked at each other for a moment, the excitement of the last three visits seeming to have drained them both equally.

"I wonder if anyone has ever told her it's bad

luck to open an umbrella indoors?" she asked Paddy. "No, I didn't think so either, boy."

Ten

By the time Liz was closing the shop for the day, the rain had eased up completely. As she walked away in the dark with Paddy by her side, she was in a considerably better mood, thanks to a kind painter who had visited an hour previously and left with four bags full of paint supplies.

Instead of her usual evening walk along the seafront, Liz decided to visit the castle for the first time since the night before Halloween. It was not that she had been avoiding it, but she had not seen the point in trying to retrace the night's events, mainly because she remembered everything first-hand.

She arrived at the castle, pleased to see Nancy already waiting for her. Without the red floodlights, the old stone structure looked even more ominous in the dark.

"Hi," Nancy said with a sheepish smile. "I'm surprised you called after last night."

"How are you feeling?"

"I've felt better," Nancy said, lowering her head. "I have a bit of a headache. I don't really remember much. Me and Polly went to the Fish and Anchor after you went home, and I'm sure I remember Shirley kicking us out at closing time."

"Misty paid me a visit this afternoon," Liz said as they linked arms and set off towards the dark courtyard. "I think you're off the hook. I can't say the same for me or Polly."

"This is why I don't drink vodka," Nancy said as she fiddled with her glasses. "It gives me silly ideas."

"Let's just forget about it."

They headed into the dark castle, Paddy trailing behind them. It was almost possible to imagine it being a different place from the one they had visited the night before Halloween. Without the hundreds of people, it felt eerily small, the silent dark swallowing them whole. Without the cushioning of the townsfolk, their steps echoed and bounced off every surface. If it was not for Nancy's companionship, Liz might have immediately turned back.

They made their way to the scene of Nathan's murder. Torn blue and white crime scene tape fluttered in the breeze, the only sign anything had happened. They walked past the tape and headed down the corridor together, just as Liz had with Simon on that night.

"Should we really be doing this?" Nancy whispered into her ear. "What if we get arrested?"

"Relax, I won't touch anything," Liz whispered back. "If they weren't finished with this place, they'd have an officer patrolling."

Not knowing what she was hoping to find, Liz walked right up to the point where she had found Nathan's headless body. As though he remembered it vividly, Paddy whimpered and pulled back.

"There's nothing here," Nancy said. "Not even a drop of blood."

"We *do* clean crime scenes."

"We?" Nancy asked with a smirk. "So much for 'ex-detective'."

"I meant they," she said quickly before handing the lead to Nancy. "Just wait here."

Liz walked forward, tracing hers and Simon's steps. She knew it was a fool's errand from the start. The police, no matter how incompetent, would not leave behind something obvious at the scene of the crime.

"We don't even know what killed him," Liz thought aloud when she returned to Nancy and Paddy. "If they'd found a murder weapon, that would be public knowledge by now."

"Must have been an axe," Nancy suggested. "Or a knife?"

"Whatever it was, it had some force behind it," Liz said, turning and looking at the spot where she had kicked Nathan's head. "It rolled all the way down there. I bet he didn't even see it coming."

"I wonder what it feels like to have your head

severed," Nancy muttered, her hand drifting up to her neck. "Your brain must know what is happening, even if your eyes don't."

"I suppose it's a quick way to go," Liz said as they walked back through the dark castle, the only light coming from the moon as it leaked through gaps in the crumbling stone. "But why decapitate him, and why that night? It's all a little obvious, don't you think?"

"Because of the legend? Maybe they wanted to blame it on the ghost?"

"Or become part of the legend?" Liz suggested as she scratched the side of her head thoughtfully. "I doubt people will ever tell the story the same way after this. Nathan will always be connected."

"But the murderer won't," Nancy said. "Surely if they wanted to be connected to the legend, they'd just confess so they could have their moment of glory?"

"The criminal mind is a strange place," Liz assured her as they walked back into the courtyard. "Believe it or not, the thrill doesn't always come from the kill, it comes from getting away with it. Like you said, the problem with that is they never get their moment of glory. I've always thought people who go to great lengths expect to be caught one day, maybe even crave it."

They walked through the courtyard towards the exit, Paddy yanking on Nancy's arm. They left the castle, both of them stopping immediately when they saw two figures looking out over the town.

"Is that -" Nancy started.

Simon quickly turned around at the sound of Nancy's voice, as did Ellie, who was clutching her big brother's hand; they had very different reactions.

"Liz!" Ellie cried, pulling away from her brother to hug Liz around the waist. "Can I stroke your dog?"

"Of course," Liz replied. "I like your coat."

"Thanks," Ellie said, standing up to show Liz her yellow raincoat. "Natasha bought it for me."

Liz gritted her jaw, forcing her lips to keep smiling. Ellie hardly had to bend to reach Paddy. They came face to face, and Paddy ran his tongue up her cheek, causing her to giggle.

"Your dog is funny," Ellie said as she wiped her cheek with her pink mitten. "I want a dog."

Liz looked up at Simon as he shuffled on the

spot uncomfortably. Liz's embarrassment at what had happened last time they had spoken made it difficult to sustain eye contact.

"Ellie, why don't we take Paddy on a little walk?" Nancy said, already grabbing the little girl's hand. "Let's give Liz and Simon a minute alone."

Nancy winked at Liz as she hurried off, her short fringe bouncing up and down above her glasses. Ellie turned back and waved at Liz before they vanished around the side of the castle.

"Ellie wanted to come and look at the view," Simon explained, his hands deep in his pockets, his chin buried in a grey scarf. "I wouldn't have brought her up here, considering what happened, but I needed to get out of the house."

"Trouble in paradise?" Liz replied, almost regretting the words the second they left her lips. "I'm sorry, I just -"

"Natasha was jilted at the altar," Simon blurted out, taking a step forward. "I tried telling you earlier, but it just wouldn't come out, and then you mentioned Fishy Chris, and then I -"

"Took your cheese back and stormed out?" A playful smirk tickled Liz's lips. "I deserved it. You were trying to make peace, and I was being my usual stubborn self."

Simon dropped his head, a soft smile taking over his lips. Something deep within Liz squirmed hard, making her want to forget everything that had happened.

"We're just friends," Simon said, echoing what he had said in the shop. "She was going to marry this city banker, and he left her at the altar. She panicked and came here. I couldn't just turn her away."

Liz nodded, wanting to believe that, but she could not shake the way Natasha looked at Simon.

"Why didn't you call me after I walked away?" Liz asked, the one question she had been craving to know the answer to. "I felt like you suddenly ditched me."

"You left," he said, his brows crinkling. "I thought you'd changed your mind about the coffee, and you didn't want to take things any further."

"Because a woman in a wedding dress was hugging you," Liz said, her voice unintentionally rising. "It felt like a clear message."

"She's not a bad person," Simon protested. "But I'm not in love with *her*."

"In *l-love*?" Liz echoed, the words scratching against her tongue. "Are you saying -"

Before Liz could finish her sentence, Paddy bolted towards her with a stick in his mouth, almost knocking her clean off her feet. Ellie ran around the corner of the castle, a gigantic grin on her face. Nancy followed seconds later, completely out of breath and less happy with the situation.

Paddy stopped and doubled around, his backside in the air, his tail wagging. Ellie pried the stick from his mouth, tossing it back towards Nancy, who quickly darted out of the way as she clutched her ribs.

"I don't know how kids do it," Nancy panted as she adjusted her glasses. "I – I can't breathe."

"I should go," Simon said after checking his phone. "A last-minute order has come through. The ice cream labels need applying."

Liz nodded her understanding, even though she wanted to grab Simon and demand to know how the sentence would have ended. They locked eyes for a moment, the cold and Ellie's joyful cries disappearing; it felt like that moment in the castle before they had found Nathan's body. Simon looked like he was about to say something else, but he took Ellie's hand, smiled a timid goodbye, and set off down the hill.

"*So?*" Nancy asked with a wide grin after catching her breath. "Did you kiss and make up?"

"Not quite," Liz said, frowning into the distance, unsure of what had just happened. "How did I get here?"

Taking a deep breath, she leaned against a wall looking over the little town. In the darkness, she looked out at the horizon, the choppy waves illuminated by the faint moon. Paddy dropped the stick at her feet before staring expectantly up at her. She kicked it feebly as she pulled her scarf tighter around her neck.

Nancy took a seat beside her, and they sat in a calm silence. Liz took the time to think about everything that had happened over the past year; she could hardly believe the changes she had undergone. She had moved to Scarlet Cove to get away from her life in Manchester, but it appeared to have followed her.

"Penny for your thoughts?" Nancy asked, nudging Liz softly with her shoulder. "What're you thinking about?"

"Nothing and everything."

"That's a little vague," Nancy replied with a creased brow. "Spill the beans, Liz. I'm your friend, aren't I?"

"Yes."

"Friends tell each other things," Nancy said with a coaxing nod. "I've seen that look before, and it's nothing to do with this Simon situation."

Liz turned to her friend with a smile. She came across as ditzy and carefree most of the time, but she was more perceptive than Liz gave her credit for.

"I was married," Liz said carefully. "For a long time."

"Did it not work out?"

"That's *one* way of putting it," Liz replied, tears gathering behind her lashes.

"What do you mean?"

Liz drew in a breath, ready to tell Nancy the secret she had vowed to leave behind in her old life.

"He died," she said before pausing. "His name was Lewis. We were both on a case, and he was shot. That was nearly three years ago, but I swear it feels like thirty."

"Oh, Liz," Nancy said, resting her hand on Liz's to give it a reassuring squeeze. "I'm so sorry."

Liz looked at Nancy as she smiled through her tears. She looked down at the hand, expecting more questions to come, but they did not. This action alone comforted Liz more than any words could. The quietness descended once more, and they both looked out at the black waves.

"For the record, Simon does really like you," Nancy said, still looking ahead. "A lot."

"Did he tell you that?"

"Not in so many words, but I can tell. He isn't like most guys. I've known him-"

"For as long as you can remember," Liz chuckled. "I know."

Nancy squeezed her hand again, only pulling away when her phone vibrated loudly in her pocket. She dug it out, her jaw dropping immediately.

"What is it?" Liz asked.

"Jack just texted me," Nancy said, turning the phone around to Liz. "He says The Sea Platter has closed down."

"But I only spoke to Daniel this afternoon," Liz said, squinting at the bright screen. "How could it have closed so quickly?"

"Beats me," Nancy shrugged. "A lot of strange things have been happening in this town recently. C'mon, let's go back. I'm freezing up here."

As they walked down into the town arm in arm with Paddy leading the way, Liz's mind whirred with questions. What could have happened for Daniel to close The Sea Platter so quickly, and was it connected to Nathan's murder? Liz was not sure, but she felt a renewed surge of energy to get to the bottom of both mysteries.

Eleven

Liz's first delivery from the new supplier arrived a few days later just before she had been about to close. After the deliveryman stacked the boxes inside the shop, she slid a craft knife across the tape, and ripped back the cardboard. She pulled out the invoice that was balancing on top, and dug through the polystyrene pellets to the oil paints. She plucked a couple out at random, pleasantly surprised by their apparent high quality despite the low price tag.

After moving the boxes into the small stock room behind the counter, she glanced over the invoice, nothing seeming out of place until the last line. Just above the final total, which only came to £76.59, there was a minus £200 'discount'.

"Odd," she whispered to herself, not remembering the supplier mentioning anything about a discount when she placed her first order on the phone.

A family she did not recognise shuffled into the shop. Liz pushed the invoice into her back pocket as she smiled at the family. She quickly learned they were in Scarlet Cove for a short autumn holiday. When they asked about the recent beheading, Liz played dumb, pretending not to know anything that had not already been mentioned on the news.

The two children picked out felt-tip pens with colouring books, and the mother picked out a bundle of wool, which she said was the perfect shade for a blanket she was knitting back home.

When she was alone in the shop once again, Liz flipped the sign, locked the door, and grabbed Paddy from upstairs. Bundled up in her scarf and gloves, she set off to the seafront, the cool early evening air calm and refreshing.

With Paddy pulling in front of her, Liz wandered aimlessly next to the sea wall, the waves crashing furiously as the sky began to darken. Paddy paused and cocked his leg against a weed that had sprung up through a crack in the pavement. Liz averted her eyes and looked in the direction of Coastline Cabaret. Two police cars were parked outside, even though the bar did not appear to have yet opened.

"Come on, boy," Liz said, tugging Paddy away from the weeds when he was finished doing his business. "Let's see what's happening."

Liz approached the bar, and considered tying Paddy to a lamppost, but decided Patsy probably would not mind her bringing him in since they had not yet opened.

Liz edged quietly through the door, glad her sudden appearance went unnoticed. She walked along the side of the room and sat down at the nearest table, Paddy close by her side.

Misty was sitting on the edge of the stage with

Derrick right next to her, his arm firmly around her shoulders. Patsy stood by chewing her nails while three officers questioned Misty. Just from the looks on their faces, Liz could tell something had happened to Misty, and that the police were there to question her as a victim, rather than a suspect. The first thought that sprang to Liz's mind was of the figure she had seen outside Misty's house.

Liz waited until the police officers snapped their notepads shut before standing up. Patsy hurried across to the bar to refill the boxes of crisps that were stacked up in the corner, but Misty and Derrick stayed exactly where they were on the stage, whispering under their breath.

"Everything okay?" Liz asked as she approached the stage. "I spotted the police outside, and I wanted to check nothing bad had happened."

"It wasn't *bad*, it was *awful!*" Misty wailed, wiping her eyes. "Someone was watching me sleep last night."

"Are you sure?" Liz asked, arching a brow.

"Yes, I'm *sure!*" the singer cried. "They were stood in the corner of my room. I thought I was imagining it at first. I thought it might have been a bad dream, but it was *real*. They were dressed completely in black. I called out, and they darted out of my bedroom, and out of the front door."

"That sounds awful," Liz said, her brows tensing. "Do the police know who it was?"

"No," Misty said, shrugging off Derrick's arm so she could jump down from the stage. "I told them that you saw a figure outside my house too. It's spooked me, alright. I've got a show tonight, and I don't know how I'm going to perform when someone wants to *kill* me!"

Liz had seen her fair share of stalker related incidents, and she knew that if someone was going to kill, they would probably not have bolted when they were caught in the middle of the night.

"You're a *star*, Misty," Derrick reminded her. "That's *how* you're going to perform. You're the *shining* star in this dark town. The people *need* you."

Misty nodded her agreement, tucking her black hair behind her ears. She inhaled deeply before puffing her chest out.

"You're right," she said with sudden determination. "I need to get ready. Maybe the scout will be coming tonight?"

"I'm almost *certain* of it," Derrick said, tapping her on the shoulder. "Tonight's *the* night you get your ticket out of here."

"I thought you said that was happening the other day?" Liz jumped in, remembering what Misty had said during her visit to the shop.

"They had to cancel," Misty said, eyeing Liz suspiciously. "It's quite common."

"Very common," Derrick said certainly. "They're busy people. Things pop up all the time."

"If they don't turn up tonight, I'm going to be *convinced* someone has put a curse on me," Misty said dramatically, clearly feeling more than a little sorry for herself. "Things have been going from bad to worse recently."

"You're a star!" Derrick reminded her once again. "Your struggles make you stronger."

Misty nodded, despite probably having heard the same clichés from Derrick more than once. Liz wondered what type of cut he took to be her talent agent, and if it was worth having him around to give the constant reassurances.

Misty went to her dressing room, leaving Derrick and Liz standing awkwardly on the dance floor. He looked down at Paddy before turning on his heels and grabbing a mop, which had been propped up against the stage. He dumped it into a rusty bucket, wrung it out, and slapped it against the wooden dance floor, the smell of disinfectant attacking Liz's senses.

Leaving Misty to get ready and Derrick to finish his mopping, she walked Paddy out of the bar, her mind whirring. Who had been watching Misty sleep, and more importantly, why? The thought of someone watching her while she slept sent a shudder down Liz's spine. Was the dark figure that she had seen the same person who had been watching Misty?

Leaving Coastline Cabaret behind, Liz and Paddy wandered further along the seafront. She walked across the wooden jetty leading to Christopher's office. He was standing on the edge looking out to sea, wearing one of his perfectly tailored suits, his back to Liz; he looked deep in thought. Liz cleared her throat.

"Elizabeth," he beamed with a grin as he turned around. "What a lovely surprise. I was a little lost in my own thoughts then. How are you?"

"I'm good," Liz said as she reached into her back

pocket. "The delivery from the suppliers you recommended arrived today. There was a huge discount added to my account."

For a brief second, Liz thought she saw a flicker of dread in Christopher's pearly eyes, but he composed himself quickly.

"It must just be a new customer discount," he said with a shaky smile. "They're not uncommon."

"I suppose," Liz said as she looked down at the invoice. "I barely paid anything for what I got. It almost feels like robbery."

"Enjoy it," he said with a wink. "It means your profit margins widen."

Liz was not going to argue with that. As she tucked the invoice in her back pocket again, she was more aware than ever that profit was important to keep her business alive.

"Do you know what happened to The Sea Platter?" Liz asked, folding her arms across her body as the wind rattled down the jetty. "I heard it had closed down."

"Oh," Christopher said, his eyes widening like a deer caught in the headlights. "You know how business is. It's tricky to survive these days."

Liz arched a brow sceptically as she tried to look Christopher in the eyes, but he could not seem to maintain her gaze for more than a second.

"You wouldn't be involved, would you?" Liz asked, not needing to be a detective to spot Christopher's obvious guilt a mile off. "You were jacking up his prices."

"It's just business," he said quickly. "If you can't compete, you shouldn't be running a business."

"With that logic, I should just shut my shop," Liz said, the invoice burning a hole in her back pocket. "You helped me out, but you kept putting Daniel's prices up because you knew he was struggling. You didn't need the money, so why did you do that?"

Christopher opened and closed his mouth like one of his own fish. He looked up and down the jetty, as though searching for a way out, but the only escape route was through Liz and Paddy, and she would not move until she had an answer. Parting her legs slightly, she steadied her stance, tucking her arms even tighter across her chest.

"I wanted to buy The Sea Platter, so I upped the prices of the fish," Christopher admitted with an apologetic shrug. "It's just business. I knew Daniel couldn't afford his bills, so I squeezed him out. When I told him about the latest increase, he shut up shop immediately. He just gave up. He doesn't understand what it takes to run a successful restaurant."

"How could you do that?" Liz scolded, her eyes creasing as she stared at Christopher. "That's despicable."

"It's not a big deal."

Liz knew Christopher could be ruthless when it came to business, but this shocked even her.

"You've just ruined a man's life," Liz spat at him. "And for what? More money?"

"I'm doing him a favour," Christopher cried, his voice deepening as he seemed to grow angry with Liz's questioning. "He couldn't handle the pressure. Maybe I'll give him a job when I reopen it. This is how the business world works, Elizabeth. Divide and conquer, and then rebuild and reap the rewards."

Liz had no clue on how she should respond to Christopher. She could never imagine a person being so cold and callous, all for the sake of money. As it turned out, however, she did not need to bother formulating a response. Heavy footprints pounded down the jetty, forcing her to turn quickly on her heels. Paddy barked, just as a brick flew through the air towards them. It crashed through the window of Christopher's office, sending glass shattering in every direction. Liz jumped back, and unwittingly into Christopher's arms.

She pulled away as she squinted into the dark while Paddy growled by her feet. Just like the night outside Misty's house, she saw a dark figure.

"What the hell?" Christopher shouted as he stared into the gloom.

Liz's police instincts kicked in the moment she heard the heavy footsteps thumping back down the jetty. Without thinking, she passed Paddy's lead to Christopher before sprinting after the assailant.

It had been a long time since she had pursued anyone on foot, and her body could feel it. She had left her gym addiction behind in the city with the rest of her baggage, and had quite enjoyed watching her body soften as she enjoyed her life a little more. She was forty-two, after all, and the thought of the six in the morning gym starts for the rest of her life had made her shudder. As she left the jetty and jumped down onto the street, she wondered if she should have perhaps dropped into the gym at least once or twice since the move.

The figure, who was dressed entirely in black, was faster than Liz. She watched them hurry under the yellow glow of the spaced apart streetlamps, never getting more than one light behind them. They zoomed past The Sea Platter and continued towards Coastline Cabaret. They suddenly cut across the road, darting in between the police cars, which were still there from their visit to talk with Misty. As though the police sensed what was happening, one of the occupants of the vehicles opened their door, knocking the brick-thrower clean off their feet. They landed on the ground with a thud, groaning as their hood fell back from their face.

"*Daniel?*" Liz cried, completely out of breath. "What are you doing?"

The three officers climbed out of their cars, all of them looking as confused as the other. Liz paused over The Sea Platter owner, clutching her ribs as her breath steadied.

"What's going on?" one of the officers asked as she reached for her handcuffs.

"I'm ex-police," Liz said. "He just tossed a brick through -"

"*My* office window!" Christopher cried as he caught up, Paddy hot on his heels. "He just *vandalised* my property!"

"You had it coming," Daniel cried as he wriggled under the force of two officers turning him around to handcuff him. "You're lucky it wasn't worse!"

"What did you think this would achieve?" Liz whispered, crouching down to his level. "Did you think you could get away with it?"

"I - I don't know," he muttered, the desperation evident in his hoarse voice. "I just wanted to hit him where he'd hurt me."

Two of the officers shoved Daniel into the back of their car, while the other pulled Christopher to one side, a notepad in his hand.

As she watched the patrol car drive away, Liz almost felt sorry for Daniel, even if it did not excuse the criminal damage. A light bulb suddenly flashed above her head, making her turn in the direction of the front doors of Coastline Cabaret. Was Daniel Misty's secret observer? Liz furrowed her brows, unsure of why The Sea Platter owner would want to stalk the singer a couple of doors down. Another light flashed above her head when she remembered something Daniel had said from his hunt for chalk that had reluctantly taken him to her shop.

"'*I went on a date with Misty when she first arrived in town*'," she whispered under her breath. "Oh, Daniel. Did you kill Nathan?"

Twelve

Liz wanted nothing more than to hide under the covers when she awoke the next morning. She groaned as she looked over at the alarm clock, knowing she only had five minutes left before she had to get up. She jumped out of bed, immediately regretting it when the chill hit her. She dressed quickly in yesterday's clothes, and cursed under her breath when she touched the cold radiator; Bob's tinkering had not been successful.

After opening the shop, the first half of her workday went by uneventfully for which she was thankful, due to having been up for most of the night scribbling down everything she had discovered in her sketchpad. Sylvia visited for her weekly supplies, and the tourist family from earlier in the week returned for more felt-tip pens after admitting they had lost them, but her morning was otherwise quiet.

After shutting the shop for her lunch break, she decided to visit Simon at the farm. Thanks to their conversation at the castle, she felt they were on slightly better terms, even if she still did not know exactly where they stood.

She took the beaten path leading up to the farm with a renewed sense of confidence. The sun was high in the sky, even if it was cold, and the rain clouds were so far in the distance, it looked unlikely they would be bothering Scarlet Cove anytime soon. When the land levelled out, bringing the farmhouse into view, Liz's confidence wavered.

"Get a hold of yourself, Elizabeth Jones," she whispered. "You're a grown woman."

As she approached the farm's metal gate, she heard Simon's unmistakable laugh, but it was followed by a softer, higher pitched one. She rested her fingers on the cold metal, using it to force herself up on her tiptoes. In the distance, she could see the chicken enclosure; Simon and Natasha were feeding the chickens. Unlike her own embarrassing encounter with the chickens on her first visit to the farm, Natasha made it look easy. She scattered the chicken feed with ease, laughing at whatever Simon was saying. Remembering what Simon had said about them just being friends, she inhaled deeply and began to unhook the gate. She stopped when she saw Simon reach out and pull a piece of straw from Natasha's hair. Liz gulped hard, putting the gate back to a locked position.

Liz was about to turn and head back towards the town, but she could not seem to move. She watched them interact for almost a whole minute, unsure of what she was looking for. They seemed to really like each other. Liz felt the green-eyed monster growing deep inside her, something she had not experienced since her teenage years.

She reminded herself of her age and how

pathetic she was being. Deciding if Simon wanted to talk to her, he would come and find her, Liz began to turn on her heels. She stopped when Natasha headed for the gate of the enclosure. As though she had known she was there, her eyes locked immediately with Liz's. She smiled, and Liz found her lips returning it, until she noticed that Natasha's was not a friendly smile; it was cold and bitter, and screamed '*I've got him*'. Natasha turned back to Simon as though she had forgotten something, her hand landing on his shoulder. She said something that caused them both to laugh again, but Liz had already seen enough.

On her lonely walk back down the beaten track, Liz wished she had brought Paddy with her, not just for companionship, but so she could use him as an excuse for her visit to the farm.

The trees lining the path whistled and swayed in the wind, shedding their vibrant gold and red leaves. It would have usually inspired Liz to take a picture to paint later, but she did not hear her muse singing to her in that moment.

When she reached the edge of town, her feet took her straight to the gallery where Nancy worked without her even realising it. She had never been one for sharing gossip with girlfriends, but she knew this was one of those times that she needed to do just that.

Nancy was in her usual spot behind the reception desk when Liz arrived. The moment she caught Liz's eyes, she seemed to notice something was wrong.

"What's got you down?" Nancy asked. "Hang on, let me guess. Would it be something to do with a certain blond farmer?"

"That obvious?"

"It's written all over your face," Nancy said with a sad chuckle. "Oh, Liz. Do you like him?"

"What?"

"Do you like him?" she repeated. "It's a simple question. Yes, or no?"

Liz was caught off guard by the blunt question. She did like Simon, but admitting that in the middle of everything seemed like a bad move. To her relief, her phone rang, providing the perfect distraction. She dove into her bag, pulling out more than her phone. The invoice from the new supplier fell out. Bending down to pick it up, she looked at the screen.

"It's Miles," Liz said as she put the phone on silent. "I'll ring him back."

"What's that?" Nancy asked, nodding to the paper in Liz's hands. "A love letter about how you want to live happily ever after with Simon, but you're too stubborn to admit it, or tell him?"

"They're just some invoices," Liz said through pursed lips, tossing the paper onto the desk as she tucked the phone back into her bag. "Check if you don't believe me."

To Liz's surprise, Nancy reached for the invoice, but Liz was just thankful the topic of conversation had changed to something she was more willing to talk about. Nancy scanned the invoice, her brows tensing together.

"I thought you said you were having trouble with prices?" Nancy muttered with a shake of her head. "These guys are really expensive, and it looks like you've got the best deal in the world."

"I work with invoices every day, and I have never seen a discount for two-hundred-pounds." Nancy handed the paper back before leaning back in her chair. "In fact, I'm sure we used to order from those guys, but we stopped because they weren't very flexible."

"Christopher put me in touch with them," Liz admitted as she tucked the invoice back into her bag. "It's not a big deal. I'm not going to turn down free stock."

"Well, obviously not," Nancy said with a chuckle. "But what if it wasn't free?"

Liz narrowed her eyes on Nancy, unsure of what she was trying to get at.

"Christopher clearly paid for most of it to get in your good books," Nancy stated in a matter-of-fact voice. "C'mon, Liz! You were a detective. It's obvious."

"Why would he do that?" Liz asked, her mind working overtime. "Why would *anyone* do that?"

"He has a thing for you. You might have batted him away, but to everyone else with eyes, it's obvious he's still got the hots for you."

"He wouldn't just throw his money around like that," Liz said with a shake of her head, unsure if she believed it, or if she just did not want to believe it. "Especially after what's just happened to The Sea Platter. He forced Daniel out for money, so why would he throw some away to help me out? He's not like that."

"I can give you some suppliers," Nancy said as she flicked through a notepad. "They might not be as cheap as Christopher made out, but I can have a look through our old invoices. We're always changing to keep the gift shop fresh."

"That would be a great help," Liz said, feeling like a fool for not pushing the issue of discount further when she had questioned Christopher about it. "Thank you."

Nancy promised to call later in the day with some contact details, so Liz quickly exited before Nancy turned the conversation back around to Simon.

As she walked down the steps of the gallery, she grew angrier and angrier with Christopher for going behind her back, but she decided to confront him about it once she had calmed down. The last thing Scarlet Cove needed was another murder when one was still unsolved. For now, she was going to the shop to hopefully rack up some more sales before the end of the day.

Hurrying across the road to Crazy Waves salon,

she spotted Polly outside, dressed more like her old self again. Her beehive was back, as was her makeup, and she was wearing a leopard print blouse, with tight black jeans.

"Hi, Polly," Liz shouted, waving as she crossed the road. "How're you doing?"

"Hi, Liz," Polly called back with a smile and a wave. "I'm okay, considering."

Polly frowned down at the ground, her thickly drawn-on brows tilting up her contoured, bronzed forehead.

"Is everything really okay?" Liz asked, deciding her shop could wait. "Why aren't you in the salon?"

"I needed some fresh air," Polly said, wrapping her arms around her body as a gust of wind brushed down the narrow street. "Mrs Burns told me about what happened with Daniel. It's shaken me up a bit, I'm not going to lie."

"About the little commotion at the harbour?" Liz asked, wondering why Polly would be so shaken up by a brick through Christopher's window. "I was there."

"No, not that," Polly said, turning to Liz to look at her through her thick, false lashes. "They've arrested him for Nathan's murder."

"*What?*"

"Apparently, he was stalking Misty, so they put two and two together and searched his place," Polly explained. "Found the murder weapon at the restaurant. Some giant axe thing, like the one the grim reaper uses."

"A scythe?" Liz mumbled, almost to herself. "It was just lying around at The Sea Platter?"

"It was in the bins. Probably thought he could get away with it being collected and sent to the landfill. Just goes to show you don't know anybody, not really. I never knew the real Nathan, and the whole town didn't know the real Daniel."

Liz took a second to absorb the second-hand information, unsure of what to say. She wanted so badly to be able to storm into the police station, flash her badge, and look at the evidence first hand. Instead, she rested her hand on Polly's shoulder, deciding not to push the subject

"Do you feel any better?" Liz asked

"I thought I would, but I don't," she said, her voice faint. "Nathan's still dead, and I still don't know how to move on with my life."

Leaving Polly to get back to work, Liz did the same. The rest of the day zoomed by; she barely remembered serving the handful of customers who entered her shop. When she was finished for the day, she hurried up to her flat.

When she was faced with a microwavable meal at her kitchen counter, she thought over everything Polly had said. Daniel being arrested for Nathan's death did make sense, especially if he had been stalking Misty. She knew Misty's rejection of Daniel after one date was almost a motive to get revenge on her new lover, even if it did not fully sit right with her. She had thought she had known Daniel, even if she had seen a different side to him when he had been drunk at the castle, and when she had pushed him about his relationship to Nathan. As Polly had said, it just went to show how she did not really know him at all.

Instead of eating her microwaved beef stew and sweet potato mash, she pushed it around the plastic tray as the steam vanished. She felt like she was missing something important, something crucial that would unlock the answer to this mess.

"Do you think he did it, boy?" Liz asked Paddy

when he wandered in from the kitchen after eating his own food. He looked up at her, his head tilted to the side. "No, me neither."

Thirteen

The next evening, Liz offered to take Nancy to Coastline Cabaret. Partly as a thank you for being such a good friend during her troubles with Simon, but also because she wanted to speak to Misty about Daniel's arrest. As usual, Liz arrived early, so she headed straight for the bar.

"I've seen you hanging around here a lot recently," Patsy said when Liz slid onto one of the empty stools. She stopped polishing, planted both hands on the bar, and arched her thin brows up her taut, smooth forehead. "You aren't going to start any trouble, are you? I heard you were some kind of detective."

"*Ex*-detective," Liz said. "Can I get two glasses of wine, please?"

Patsy shrugged before grabbing two glasses and filling them with wine. After paying, Liz took the two glasses to find a seat at one of the tables. It was not that she felt uncomfortable around Patsy because she could not blame her for being a little on edge; her business neighbour had just been arrested for murder. As she found a free table, Nancy hurried in, unravelling her scarf as she looked around for Liz.

"Sorry I'm late!" Nancy cried, gratefully accepting the glass of wine. "I had to stay at the gallery to sign for an order."

"Did you hear about Daniel?" Liz asked.

"Never thought he had it in him," Nancy said with bafflement. "I always thought he was so nice. And that crazy axe thing they found in his restaurant's bin! Who would have thought it was *him*? It's all everyone is talking about."

"Word travels fast around here."

"Gossip is the best pastime we've got," Nancy said with a devilish smile. "It comes in handy at times."

Liz sipped her wine as she stared at the darkened stage. She knew the danger gossip could do to a case, especially in small towns where everyone believed every piece of information that was passed around. Liz wondered if the police took the gossip for fact because they had nothing else to go on.

"I don't think Daniel did it," Liz said. "In fact, I'm almost certain he's innocent of everything aside from lobbing a brick through Christopher's window."

"I thought you'd be happy it was all over?"

"It's all over if the *right* person is arrested and charged."

"But it *has* to be him," Nancy insisted before taking a deep gulp of wine. "It all makes sense. He was jealous of Nathan, and he's been stalking Misty."

"I understand the reasoning, but I just know it wasn't him," Liz said, knowing she was beginning to sound crazy. "Let's call it a detective's hunch."

"*Ex*-detective," Nancy reminded her with a wink. "Is that why you asked me here? Is there more investigating to be done?"

"I wanted a drink with my best friend," Liz said with a casual shrug. "*But* if we talk to Misty before we go, I wouldn't be mad about it."

"I get a night out," Nancy exclaimed, tipping her glass to Liz. "And free wine! I would be home alone otherwise. Jack has gone up to see Simon for a boys' night, although I imagine Natasha will be hovering around them, wiping up their crumbs and dabbing their chins when they dribble beer."

Liz imagined how different her life in Scarlet Cove would have been if she had not bumped into Nancy on her first day in town. She had not expected to find any friends; in fact, she had been looking forward to leading a solitary life where she did not have to pretend she was having fun in overpriced cocktail bars. She had come to Scarlet Cove to enjoy the peace and to paint, but since there was not much peace and she had not found much time to paint recently, she was glad she had a friend like Nancy.

"While we're on the subject of Daniel, did I ever

mention he and Polly went on a couple of dates when she moved here?"

"I had no idea," Liz said, frowning as she placed her wine on the table. "I would say they're a strange match, but her and Nathan were even stranger."

"I guess they just decided they were better as friends. I thought they were pretty chummy, but after everything that's unravelled, maybe I was wrong. Daniel always seemed to be looking for 'the one'. He was always dating someone, but it never went anywhere."

"That explains how he ended up on a date with Misty."

"He's quite confident when it comes to the ladies," Nancy said as her finger circled the rim of her wine glass. "He'd walk up to women and flat-out ask them if they wanted to go out sometime. He did it to me once, but I couldn't stop laughing because I've known him since school. Most of the time, the women said yes because he was so charming."

"Doesn't strike you as someone who would stalk and murder, does it?"

"Could the police really be *that* wrong?" Nancy asked, a hint of disbelief in her voice. "I thought we could trust them?"

"It's not unheard of that they'll put two and two together and get five," Liz said, knowing all too well how wrong the police could get it, especially when pressure was being put on them by the media. "And if he *was* stalking Misty, it doesn't mean he chopped Nathan's head off. I saw him that night, and he was drunk. Scythes are heavy. I don't think a drunk man could have knocked another man's head clean off."

"So, you're saying someone framed him?"

"It's not unheard of."

"But why?"

"I don't know," Liz admitted, rubbing between her brows as the chatter grew in the bar. "Opportunity, perhaps? Polly didn't have a bad word to say about Daniel when she told me he had been arrested for murdering Nathan. I don't think she believes he did it either."

The lights suddenly dimmed, and unenthusiastic applause echoed around the bar. It was a lot busier than it had been on Liz's last visit, and she cynical enough to think it was because people wanted to get a look at the woman involved in the murder case.

"I wonder what it will be today," Nancy whispered as she reluctantly clapped her hands together.

"Maybe it will be her looking in a mirror for an hour, wondering how she got so beautiful?"

"She does seem good at it," Nancy agreed, holding her hand to her mouth to stifle the giggles. "Oh, Liz, you can be wicked sometimes."

The curtains opened, a single spotlight illuminating the centre of the stage. Misty stepped out from the dark, as beautiful as always. Her floor-length black gown hugged every contour of her body, and her black hair was rolled off her face, letting her pale skin and blood-red lips draw the attention.

Misty smiled into the crowd as the applause died down. Liz noticed that she did not seem as enthusiastic as the other times she had seen her on the stage. Misty glanced to the side of the stage, nodding to someone in the wings. Liz craned her neck, spotting Derrick giving her a thumbs up. 'Defying Gravity' from Wicked started to play, causing Misty to inhale deeply ready to sing the first note. The momentum built, the anticipation palpable in the air. Liz even found herself on the edge of her seat waiting to hear Misty sing. Just as she opened her mouth, ready to hit the first note, the music cut off, along with the lights. A groan of disappointment rattled around the bar.

"What happened?" Nancy whispered.

"I don't know," Liz replied. "Maybe a fuse tripped? I don't think Misty is safe though."

The chatter grew louder and louder in the bar as phone screens began to illuminate small pockets in the gloom. The white glowing light was enough to see that Misty had vanished from the stage.

"It's alright everyone," Patsy called as she hurried around the bar with a torch. "I think a fuse has blown. I'll get it sorted. If you stay where you are, there's a free round of drinks in it for everyone."

The angry chatter died down at the promise of a free drink. Liz, on the other hand, had other things on her mind.

"C'mon," Liz said, grabbing Nancy's hand. "Let's find Misty."

Leaving their wine behind, they weaved in and out of the tables towards the dark corridor leading to Misty's dressing room.

"I don't like this," Nancy murmured. "I don't like this at all."

"I won't let anything happen to you," Liz assured her, squeezing her arm slightly. "You can go back if you want."

"And leave you?" Nancy countered, forcing a laugh. "Fat chance."

They continued down the dark corridor, Liz's fingers dragging across the wall. She counted the doors as she went, pausing when she reached the one she remembered as Misty's dressing room. She squinted into the dark, sure she could see the glittery star on the door.

"Liz?" Nancy whispered as she tugged on her arm. "W-What's that?"

"What's what?"

"That." Liz could just make out Nancy's finger as she lifted it shakily, pointing towards a slightly open door.

Liz strained her eyes into the darkness. Just as Nancy had, she saw a faint flickering light through the gap in the door.

"Do you think it's Patsy?" Nancy asked. "Fixing the fuses?"

"It looks like a candle."

Liz let go of Nancy and headed to the door. It opened with a loud creak, revealing a wooden staircase. Cold air drifted up from the darkness, tickling Liz's face. She pushed her foot onto the top step to make sure it could take her weight. It creaked loudly, but it held. Not thinking twice, Liz began her descent towards the flickering light.

"You can't be serious?" Nancy cried, yanking Liz back. "We don't know what's down there."

"Stay there," Liz said, tugging her arm free. "I'm just checking it out."

"A serial killer could be down there," Nancy protested. "But I don't want to wait here on my own. If I die, I'm coming back to haunt you."

Fear knotted her insides as they carefully made their way down the squeaky staircase. She had no idea what she was going to find, if anything at all, but she had a feeling the candle was leading her towards something relevant. They reached the bottom, the air thick with damp; Liz was sure she was going to choke.

"*Hello?*" she called down another corridor with even more doors. "Is anyone down here?"

Liz's voice bounced back at her. The candle sparkled at the end of the corridor, its flame flickering and bouncing on a small table in what looked like a cleaning supplies cupboard.

"What is it?" Nancy whispered, her nails digging into Liz's arm. "We're about to be sacrificed. I knew it. Why didn't I go to church more?"

Clutching Nancy's hand firmly in hers, Liz set off towards the candle; she did not admit she was holding her friend's hand as much for herself as she was for Nancy.

When they reached the half-open door, Liz had not been prepared for what confronted them. Liz gasped, goose bumps creeping up her arms as the hairs stood on end.

"Oh my God," Nancy muttered. "What the -"

Liz looked down at the tall candle on the table, which was surrounded with layers and layers of solid wax, concrete drips of the stuff dangling off the edge. Liz plucked the candle from its resting place, and held it up to the walls. Fear knotted inside her as a shiver of panic tingled across her shoulders.

"It's a shrine," Liz said, her eyes dancing over the walls, which were completely covered in photos of Misty Rivers.

Nancy took a step back, but Liz took one forward. She drifted the orange glow across the collage of pictures. She recognised some of them as the same headshots framing Misty's mirror, but most of them were more candid and disturbing. There were pictures of Misty eating, pictures of her singing, and even pictures of her sleeping.

"What is this place?" Nancy said, her voice hitching. "It's *sick*."

Liz's throat was completely dry; she could not speak. In the mass of pictures, she spotted a shelf of glass jars, the contents disturbing her even more than the photos. Clumps of jet-black hair filled each jar, and she did not need to be an ex-detective to know who the hair had belonged to. Below that shelf, there was another filled with costume jewellery, along with an empty bottle of perfume. Liz leaned in, the familiar sickly sweet scent still lingering on the nozzle.

"There's a padlock on the door," Nancy said. "It's usually locked up."

Liz stepped back and placed the candle back on the table, knowing the fewer things she touched, the better. Something underneath the table caught her attention; a thick scrapbook.

"Liz," Nancy said, resting her hand on Liz's shoulder. "Let's go."

Liz reached into her coat pocket and pulled out her winter gloves. She slid them on before reaching for the book. She opened the first page, and almost stopped breathing altogether. She scanned the first page as she attempted to steady her erratic pulse.

"It's Nathan," Nancy whispered as she looked down at the picture. "Who did this?"

Liz stared at the picture of Polly's boyfriend. A huge red cross had been scratched over his face in red pen, almost ripping through to the next page. Compelled to see more, she carried on turning the pages. There were various newspaper clippings from the local paper detailing the case. On the final page, there was a picture of Daniel, which looked like it had been snapped through his restaurant window. Liz was surprised to see that she was also in the picture, along with Christopher. A red circle had been drawn around Daniel's face, and a question mark over the top of Liz's frizzy red hair.

"It all makes sense," Liz said, stepping out of the

room as she pulled her phone from her pocket. "I know who killed Nathan. I can't believe I didn't see this. I need to research something to prove it."

"What?" Nancy asked, edging forward. "What is it?"

"Ever heard of a man called Gary Crabtree?" Liz asked. "I think it all hinges on him."

Fourteen

The single light bulb fizzed into life as they hurried back down the narrow corridor. She looked back at the shrine, hoping it would be less sinister in the light; it was not.

They headed towards the wooden stairs hand in hand. Nancy tripped, dragging Liz's arm back. Something metal clattered, and water splashed against Liz's shoes.

"Are you okay?" Liz asked.

"Yeah, I'm fine," Nancy said, steadying herself. "This stupid mop bucket was in the way. Let's go."

After taking the steps two at a time, they hurried past Misty's dressing room and back into the bar, where Misty had resumed her set. Liz looked around the bar, everything appearing to be back to normal, but she felt like they were in a different reality, the basement nothing but a nightmare.

Still hand in hand, they resumed their seats at their table, their wine exactly where they had left it. Nancy was about to take a sip of hers, but Liz put her hand over the top.

"*Never* leave a drink unattended," Liz said. "Especially not in here."

"I need something for my nerves, Liz," Nancy said, her hands trembling. "I'm so freaked out. We need to go to the police."

"They'll find a way to pin it on Daniel," Liz said with a shake of her head. "If they've already charged him, it will take a miracle to make them back track."

"So, we're going to wait for a miracle?"

"We're going to get a confession." Liz stood up, grabbing the two glasses of wine. "Stay here and don't move. I'll get you something stronger."

Liz took the two glasses of wine back to the bar. While Patsy served a man at the other side of the bar, Liz poured the wine into the beer drip tray. She slid onto one of the stools and pulled out her purse, her hands trembling as much as Nancy's. She turned to glance at the stage, hoping Misty would stop singing soon so they could talk, but her eyes landed on Christopher. Her blood boiled, but for an entirely different reason.

"I thought I'd find you in here," Christopher said, a confident smile plastered across his face. "What's wrong? You look like you've seen a ghost."

"What's wrong?" she echoed, feeling every ounce of anger from the past few days building up at once. "I'll tell you what's wrong, Christopher. I found out about your little deal with those suppliers you suggested. Did you think I wouldn't find out?"

Patsy walked over but immediately turned on her heels when she saw the look on Liz's face.

"Now isn't the time, Elizabeth," Christopher hissed, his eyes darting around the bar. "I was *trying* to do you a favour."

"Now is the *perfect* time," she said, making no

effort to lower her voice. "I'm not some damsel in distress you can just throw money at to impress."

"I was trying to help."

"But I didn't ask for your help," Liz snapped, her face burning. "A favour is one thing, but going behind my back to fill up my account with the cash you took from Daniel?"

"He's a murderer," Christopher said with a dry laugh. "How are you still defending him?"

"You are just like my parents," Liz said, ignoring his comment about Daniel. "If you can't fix a problem, you just throw money at it, hoping it goes away. I wanted to succeed by *myself*. It's my problem, not yours."

The silence stretched out between them, Christopher staring at her like a wounded puppy. She could feel the eyes of onlookers looking in her direction.

"I'm sorry," he whispered, his voice cracking a little. "I – I thought I was doing the right thing."

His eyes dropped to the ground, making Liz instantly feel guilty for her outburst. She blinked hard, forcing herself to remember that he had gone behind her back, but now that she was looking at him, a part of her wanted to believe that his intentions had been pure.

"I'll be using a different supplier from now on," Liz said after a calming breath. "I'll also be returning the money."

Christopher nodded glumly, looking like a child who had just been scolded for taking one too many biscuits from the jar. Instead of trying to defend himself, he turned on his heels and headed straight for the door.

"What was that about?" Nancy asked after hurrying over. "Did you confront him?"

"I think I was too harsh," Liz said as she tried to catch Patsy's attention to order their drinks. "He says he was just trying to do me a favour."

"It doesn't matter," Nancy said as she adjusted her glasses. "We have bigger fish to fry than Fishy Chris. Misty has finished singing."

Liz glanced over Nancy's shoulder, surprised to see the stage empty. She had been so wrapped up in her argument with Christopher, she had not noticed that the music had stopped.

She turned back to the bar to tell Patsy she did not want to order after all, but she was already holding two glasses of wine in her hands.

"You look like you need these," Patsy said as she handed the glasses over. "On the house."

Nancy gulped down her wine in seconds, but Liz's stomach was too unsettled. She took a sip, leaving it on the bar when Patsy turned away.

"Come on," Liz said. "We need to talk to Misty."

"Okay," Nancy said, pausing to burp up the wine. "I needed that."

They hurried through the bar, which seemed to be emptying quickly now that Misty had finished singing. When they were back at the entrance to the corridor, Liz felt disturbing quakes in her serenity when she looked at the door leading to the cellar.

"Maybe we *should* call the police?" Nancy whispered as they made their way towards Misty's dressing room. "This doesn't feel right."

"Trust me," Liz said. "I just need to talk to Misty to clear something up first."

Nancy clung to Liz's coat as they slipped into the room. As usual, Misty was sitting in front of the mirror, admiring herself as she wiped off her red lipstick.

"Do you *mind?*" Misty snapped, twisting in her chair, the tight dress making her movements awkward. "Why are you always in my reflection these days? You're like my shadow!"

Misty spun back to the mirror, waving her hand as if telling them to leave. Liz straightened her spine, shook off Nancy, and stepped forward into the glow of Misty's vanity bulbs.

"Misty, this is serious," Liz said. "It's *very* serious."

"How can anything *serious* still be happening?" she shrieked, her hand slipping so that red lipstick smeared down her porcelain-white chin. "My stalker is behind bars, my lover is still dead, and you're *still* bugging me."

Liz looked deep into Misty's eyes via the reflection; it became obvious that she really did believe that Daniel was her stalker.

"Why are you so sure Daniel was the one who was watching over you when you slept?" Liz asked, resting her hands on the back of Misty's chair. "Did you see him?"

"I've already told you!" Misty cried, tossing her makeup wipe onto the cluttered dressing table. "I saw a man dressed in black watching over me."

"But you didn't see Daniel specifically?"

"Well, no," Misty said, her finely drawn brows pinching together. "But you were the one who chased him after he smashed Christopher's window. You *saw* him. The police found the murder weapon in *his* bin. I was lucky I wasn't the next victim."

"You were never going to be a victim," Liz said. "Not of murder, at least. You *are* one of the victims in all of this, but this whole thing has revolved around you."

"Just like she thinks the whole world does," Nancy mumbled from behind Liz.

Misty craned her neck around Liz to send daggers in Nancy's direction.

"What do I have to do with Daniel smashing a window?" Misty asked. "I don't even know that fish man."

"Well, that's the one thing that isn't a part of all this," Liz clarified, nodding carefully in the mirror. "But that incident made Daniel visible, meaning that the real killer could easily frame him. You saw a dark figure, and Daniel was arrested in all black. It was too perfect."

"But he was obsessed with me," Misty cried, shaking her head at Liz. "After I rejected him, he couldn't accept it, so he tried to scare me."

"That doesn't sound like Daniel," Nancy muttered. "He was a serial dater. You were just a blip on his radar. He moved on quicker than a horse at the races."

"I don't understand," Misty snapped, her hands disappearing up into her perfectly lacquered hair. "What are you saying?"

Liz took in a deep breath, knowing the next thing she was going to say was likely to be met with stiff resistance.

"What do you know about Derrick?" Liz asked. "What do you *really* know about him?"

"Why are you asking about Derrick?" Misty replied, her patience seeming to be growing thin. "He's my agent."

"When did you first meet him?"

"Here," Misty said, suddenly standing up so that she was face to face with Liz in her stilettos. "I moved to Scarlet Cove, got the job here, and he offered to represent me. After I found out about his brother in London, I knew it was meant to be."

"Derrick was just a cleaner here, wasn't he?" Liz asked, her voice trembling. "A cleaner who saw a pretty girl with big dreams and knew what to say."

"I don't understand what you're -"

Before Liz could finish her sentence, a loud yelp from behind made them both turn around. In the doorway of the dressing room, Derrick had appeared, his arm suddenly around Nancy's neck. His eyes were wide behind his thick glasses, and his wispy strands of remaining hair stood on end, his bald scalp glowing in the soft light.

"*Derrick?*" Misty cried. "What are you doing?"

"Don't move," Derrick cried, his arm tightening around Nancy's throat. "I could snap her neck in seconds, and I will if I need to."

Looking deep into Nancy's terrified eyes, Liz raised her hands above her head. Misty did not follow suit, instead choosing to stare at the man she had trusted for years.

"What are you *doing?*" Misty cried. "Derrick, you're scaring me!"

"No more games, Misty," Derrick cried, a dry smirk taking over his lips. "The time has come. It's time for us to leave this stupid town so we can be together. We'll get rid of these two, and run off to London. I'll make you a star like I promised!"

Derrick's arm tightened harder around Nancy's neck, causing her to shiver in pain. She writhed against him, attempting to break free as blood rushed to her round cheeks. Tears trickled from her tight eyes.

"You don't want to do this," Liz said cautiously, her hands still up. "Just let her go, and we'll talk."

"Talk about what?" he sneered, taking a step back and dragging Nancy with him. "You've ruined everything! I saw you in the cellar. I heard you coming, so I hid in the barrel room. Why couldn't you just stay out of things and leave us alone?"

"What are you talking about?" Misty screamed, her emotions growing out of control. "Will somebody explain to me what is happening right now? I demand to know."

"There's nothing I couldn't give you, Misty," Derrick cried, his eyes growing wide as he smiled at the singer. "All you have to do is ask. I've already done so much for you. Nathan was never good enough for you. He dimmed your sparkle, so I got rid of him for you so you could soar."

The penny dropped, causing Misty's jaw to slacken. She stumbled forward, using Liz's shoulder to steady herself.

"Tell me it isn't true, Derrick?" Misty croaked, her voice barely audible. "You wouldn't do something like that."

"It was almost too easy," he stated, no remorse in his voice. "Remember last year's Halloween show when we re-enacted the beheading? Oh, you were marvellous in that. You showed your talent that night. We still had the props lying around. I didn't even mean to order a real scythe, but I kept hold of it, just in case. When I caught you and Nathan in here the week before Halloween, I *knew* I had to *fix* this. I *knew* it wasn't the *real* you. I *knew* you would never hurt me like that. Oh, I sorted it out all right, and it was child's play. The second I saw Daniel being arrested outside, I ran around the back and dumped the murder weapon in his bin. I knew it would only be a matter of time until the police got the wrong end of the stick."

"How did you know Nathan would be at the castle?" Liz asked, her eyes trained on Nancy as her red face began to turn a ghostly white. "Lucky guess?"

"I went to the salon to book Misty in for a trim," Derrick said, his eyes lighting up as though he was pleased with himself. "You were right about Polly, Misty. She really is a bimbo. All I had to do was ask if she'd be at the castle, and she blurted out that she was going with her boyfriend."

"Just let go of Nancy so we can talk about this properly," Liz pleaded as Nancy's lashes began to flutter. "She has nothing to do with this."

"You *know* it was me," he shot back, his grip tightening. "I can't let either of you go now. This is how it has to be."

"*Derrick!* Stop this now," Misty cried, her voice similar to that of a scared child. "Liz is right. This isn't Nancy's fight."

"The minute I saw you I knew," Derrick whispered, a smile tickling his lips. "I knew you were the only one for me."

Misty looked desperately at Liz. Not knowing what to say or do, she searched through her brain for what to do in a hostage situation. She had only been involved in two in her whole career, but she had had support from her colleagues. With Misty's acid-tongue, Liz knew their chances were slim.

"Don't look at her," Derrick hissed, staring at Misty. "Look at me. You belong to me. We belong to each other. I have helped you become who you are. You're my shining star, Misty. The only star bright enough in the sky to sparkle in the darkness."

Nancy had completely sagged in Derrick's arms; she had stopped weeping. The lights surrounding the vanity mirror fizzed and hissed, dimming and brightening up again.

"They do that sometimes," Misty explained quickly, as though the trivial matter was suddenly important. "I can't remember how many times I've asked Patsy to look at them."

Liz stared at Nancy's limp body, knowing time was running out. She looked around the room, hoping to see something she could use to attack Derrick. She spotted a collection of stiletto heels, wondering if she could get across the room quickly enough without startling him; she knew it was unlikely.

As though the Gods were shining down on her in that moment, one of the bulbs popped, shattering glass across the dressing table. Misty screamed out, jumping across the room. It was enough to startle Derrick, weakening his grip around Nancy's neck.

Liz did not waste another second. She dove forward, dragging Nancy out of the man's arms. She flung Nancy across the room, silently apologising for the rough move in her head. Derrick's hand struck her face, forcing Liz to stumble back. She clutched her cheek, strands of her frizzy red hair strewn across her face. All of her police training vanished, instead being replaced with her primal instincts. With a single, swift, sharp kick, she sent the tip of her shoe up between Derrick's legs.

The cleaner immediately dropped to his knees with a grunt, clutching his crotch. He sagged to the side, his eyes bulging as his face reddened like Nancy's had. Liz's fists clenched by her sides, but she resisted the urge to plant her knuckles in the middle of his face.

"Pass me something to tie his arms up," Liz commanded. "*Quickly!*"

Misty looked around her dressing room, her fingers clenching a fistful of her hair. After a second of panic, she scrabbled through one of her brimming drawers. Settling on a sparkly, sickly green leotard, she finally tossed it to Liz. Straddling him with her knees, her training suddenly rebooting, she tied his hands securely behind his back.

"Call the police!" Liz ordered. "And an ambulance."

Misty nodded before rummaging through the makeup on her dressing table for her mobile phone. Liz hurried to Nancy's side, just as she began to cough and splutter, the colour flooding her cheeks in an instant.

"Are you okay?" Liz asked.

Nancy did not speak, instead nodding through hoarse coughs. Liz let out a relieved sigh as she looked back at Derrick. He attempted to stagger up to his feet, but before he could, Misty sent a jewellery box crashing down on his head.

"What the *hell* just happened?" Misty cried, the jewellery box falling to the ground with Derrick, costume jewellery spilling out around him. "How did you know it was him?"

"I didn't until today," Liz admitted as she rubbed Nancy's arm. "When the power cut out, we came looking for you to ask you why you thought Daniel was your stalker. We saw a flickering candle, so we followed it. When was the last time you visited the basement?"

"Never," Misty admitted. "Derrick said it was a horrid place full of damp."

"It is," Liz said with a nod. "But there's also a shrine down there. A shrine dedicated to you. Someone has been collecting pictures of you for a long time, as well as other things."

"What other things?"

"Jewellery, parts of your costumes," Liz paused, unsure if she should continue. "Hair."

"Oh, God." Misty stumbled back into her chair, her hand firm against her cheek. She looked as though she was about to gag. "You mean Derrick is the person you saw outside my house, and the person I caught watching me sleep?"

"I knew the shrine could have belonged to a number of people, but I remembered seeing Derrick mopping the dance floor, which I had thought was strange for a talent agent. It was all too perfect. The door had a padlock on it, but he seemed to be using the darkness to pay his creation a little visit."

"Why would he do this?" Misty whispered, looking up at her reflection in the mirror. "He promised me so much. I believed him."

"That was something I didn't understand," Liz said, pulling her phone from her pocket. "Not until I researched it online. I didn't understand why Derrick would do all of this if he really could give you the stardom he promised."

"But his brother?" Misty said. "Gary. He's real. I've seen his business card."

"He *was* real," Liz said, handing the phone to Misty. "Gary Crabtree jumped off Westminster Bridge five years ago. His body washed up on the bank of the Thames in July 2012. He *did* work in the West End, and he *was* a powerful director, but there was nothing he could have done for your career from beyond the grave."

"My dreams," Misty said, her eyes wide as she stared down at her makeup. "I thought I was going places."

"There were no auditions or scouts. Derrick lied to you, and I suspect he would have kept lying to you until you started to suspect things. I dread to think what he would have done then."

"I did it -" Derrick croaked, his lids half-closed. "I did it because I love you, and I know you love -"

"Don't you *dare* finish that sentence," Misty cried, jumping up again. "You're crazy, I thought you were going to *help* me. Do you really think I would have looked twice at you if I didn't think you were connected? Look at yourself, Derrick. People like you don't end up with girls like me. You're a fat, old, cleaner. I'm the *star*, remember?"

Liz sighed, wondering if Misty had learned anything from the sorry episode. When she heard police sirens in the distance, she helped Nancy up to her feet, relieved that it was all over.

Leaving Misty in the dressing room with Derrick, Liz helped Nancy down the corridor as police officers hurried down the corridor, batons in hand.

"He's in there," Liz said. "You might want to charge Daniel with vandalising Christopher Monroe's office, not that I think Christopher will want to take things any further. Your real murderer is tied up in a green leotard."

Liz emerged from the corridor and into the bar. She sat Nancy in the nearest chair, waving over the paramedics as they rushed in. The remaining customers in the bar looked at each other, no one seeming to know what was happening.

"Liz?" Misty asked when she joined them in the bar. "Is this all my fault?"

Liz thought for a moment. Although she could blame her for breaking Polly's heart, the blame had to lie entirely with Derrick. As much as she disliked the woman, she could not live with herself if she let her think she was responsible.

"Derrick is a sick man," she said, stepping away from Nancy as the paramedics started to check her over. "If you want to be a star, make it happen on your own. You can't learn to paint a beautiful picture without getting a little paint on your clothes."

Misty frowned at Liz as though she had no idea what she was suggesting. Not caring either way, Liz sat next to Nancy and clutched her hands.

"Maybe next time, you stay outside?" Liz said with a soft smile.

Fifteen

"Three cheers to Liz!" Nancy exclaimed, her head wobbling above her thick neck brace.

"*Three cheers*," the rest of the Fish and Anchor chorused, raising their drinks to Liz.

News of Liz's discovery had spread like wildfire in the days since Derrick's arrest, causing everyone to gather in the local pub to congratulate her, and no doubt to hear the gossip first hand. As it turned out, most people had never even heard of Derrick, and there were even people who did not know Coastline Cabaret had a singer.

Liz finished the rest of her wine, and was about to ask Shirley, the tough landlady, for a refill, but she felt someone tap her lightly on the shoulder. Liz turned with a smile, wondering who wanted to hear the story of the shrine now; her smile dropped when she saw that it was Natasha.

"Can I have a word?" Natasha asked with a gentle smile. "In private?"

Unsure of what she could possibly want to talk about, Liz reluctantly followed Natasha into a quiet corner of the pub. She looked over at Nancy, who could only offer an awkward shrug with her restrained neck.

"I'm sorry about everything," Natasha whispered as she picked at her nails awkwardly. "I didn't mean to barge in on Simon's life like this. I had no idea he was seeing someone. I would never have come back if I had known, but once I was here, it was easy to slip back into my old place."

"We were never together," Liz corrected her. "Not really."

"Neither were Simon and I," Natasha said with a sad smile. "Well, not since we were kids. I tried. Believe me, I tried. He's the nicest guy I've ever known."

Natasha paused to look across the bar at Simon, who was chatting with Jack. She sighed heavily, before finally looking Liz in the eyes.

"I was jilted," Natasha started. "He was a city lawyer, and I thought I loved him. I thought he loved me too, but he didn't seem to feel the same, especially when I told him about this the night before the wedding."

Natasha rested her hand on her stomach, tears welling up along her lashes.

"If it makes you feel any better, Simon isn't interested in reliving the past," Natasha said as she rubbed her stomach. "I think I had this delusion that he'd open his arms and we could become a happy family overnight. He knew that, and he told me it wasn't going to happen on that first night, but he's such a good guy, he still helped me."

The sincerity in Natasha's voice made Liz's doubts melt away instantly. The space left behind by the doubts was quickly filled with embarrassment.

Why had she acted like such a jealous woman without having heard the full story?

"I'm sorry," Natasha said, her hand on Liz's shoulder. "You deserve him, Liz. I don't think you should have put up with me acting the way I have."

Liz accepted Natasha's apologies with a soft smile. The woman walked away, her hand resting on her tummy. Simon had been right; she was not so bad after all.

***

AFTER ANSWERING THE SAME QUESTIONS repeatedly as vaguely as she could, the buzz finally calmed down, leaving her able to sit with her friends without interruption.

"I can't believe that guy has a shrine," Jack cried with a shake of his head before he sipped some of his favourite Scarlet Cove Brew. "An *actual* shrine!"

"It was like something out of a horror film," Nancy replied before Liz could get a word in. "There were pictures of Misty *everywhere*, he even had some of her hair. *Her hair*! If I never see that place again as long as I live, I'll die happy."

"I bet Simon has one dedicated to Liz," Jack winked in Simon's direction. "In fact, I think I might have seen it."

Simon tossed a scrunched-up napkin at Jack, his face turning bright red with embarrassment. Jack gave Simon a playful wink before hooking his arm around Nancy's shoulder, making sure to be careful around her neck.

"Is there any permanent damage?" Natasha asked after sipping her orange juice. "It looks sore."

"The doctors said it was just bruising," Nancy said, her hand drifting up to the white brace. "I wasn't really listening. I was too busy thanking God that I was alive."

"You must have been so scared," Natasha added.

"I thought I was done for," Nancy said uncomfortably. Jack sensed this and rubbed her arm. "If it hadn't been for Liz, I dread to think what would've happened."

"You wouldn't have been in that situation in the first place," Liz reminded her.

"You're a true hero, Liz," Jack said. "Don't forget that."

Liz blushed, and she suddenly felt Simon's eyes

on her. He smiled, as though he was the proudest person in the world.

"I just did what anybody else would have done," she said with a shrug. "Detective Jones takes over sometimes."

"You're too modest," Simon said.

Liz smiled at him, their eyes locking for a few moments before she was interrupted by a familiar voice.

"Elizabeth?" Christopher said before clearing his throat. "Can I talk to you, please?"

Liz looked at all of her friends who all nodded their approval, aside from Simon who stayed motionless. Deciding they still had unfinished business, Liz excused herself after a quick sip of wine.

Christopher headed to the front door, looking as uncomfortable as he possibly could in the foreign surroundings. The cold whipped around Liz's loose hair as soon as she opened the door, sending it across her face. She shivered as she tucked the strands behind her ears. They stood silently in the dark for a moment, both looking ahead at her shop across the square.

"I'm sorry," Christopher said abruptly as he rubbed the creases on his high forehead. "I was only trying to help."

"I know," Liz replied. "And now that I've had time to clear my head, I know you weren't trying to be malicious. Not to me, at least. My shop, it's just something I *need* to do on my own. I'm sorry for shouting at you."

"It's okay. I should have known really." Christopher sighed as he glanced up at the almost full moon in the sky. "Daniel and I are going into business together with The Sea Platter. I realised how terrible I'd been, so I made him an offer, and he accepted. We've smoothed things over, and we're both really excited about the future. With his cooking skills and my business brain, we'll be unstoppable."

"That's great," Liz said, a genuine smile filling her lips. "See how much nicer it feels when you help build people up instead of '*dividing and conquering*'? After everything Daniel has been through, the poor guy deserves some success."

"He owes that fresh start to you," Christopher said, proving that the rumour mill even stretched as far as Christopher's office at the harbour. "I'm glad to see you're still in one piece. You seem to have quite a knack for solving mysteries."

"I hope it's the last mystery I have to dive into," Liz said firmly. "I'd like to get back to my painting."

"And you will," Christopher said, stretching out his hand. "I wasn't planning on sticking around. Daniel and I have a lot of things to go over."

"Goodnight, Christopher," Liz said as she accepted his handshake. "It takes a good man to admit when he's made a mistake. Apology accepted."

Liz felt much lighter when Christopher walked away. She looked at her shop again, even more determined to make a success out of her little arts and crafts business. Walking backwards to the edge of the market square, she craned her neck to look up at the castle on the hill. It stood proudly, casting its shadow over Scarlet Cove for another year. Liz did not doubt she would be there next year to indulge in the legend again; she just hoped the beheading would stay in the stories from now on.

"It really is something, isn't it?" Natasha said softly, startling Liz as she walked out of the pub. "I used to love going up there as a kid. I always wanted to be the princess in the castle."

"I think I'd end up being the cook," Liz said with a chuckle. "Which is funny considering I can't cook."

"Neither can I," Natasha admitted. "Have you tried Simon's cheese pie? It only takes one bite to remind me of home. I've lived in so many different places since leaving here, and nowhere has felt like home since. I'm going to miss it."

"Aren't you staying?"

"No," she said with a heavy shake of her head. "My mum has offered for me to stay with her until I've figured out my next step. I'm leaving tomorrow. I think I've more than overstayed my welcome."

Side by side, they looked up at the castle in the dark. Even though they were in silence, Liz felt like they had more in common than she would have ever thought. Liz had left the place she had thought was her home to find her true place in the world, and she knew Natasha would do that too.

"You have a good thing with Simon," Natasha said, breaking the silence. "You seem to make him happy."

"I do?"

"He talks about you constantly. I think he's head over heels."

Liz smiled to herself, glad that the wind broke her hair free to cover her blushing cheeks.

"I'd better get back to the farm," Natasha said, stepping backwards into the road. "I have a lot of packing to do before my train. Goodbye, Liz."

"Bye," Liz said, waving delicately at the woman she had spent the past week subconsciously hating. "Have a good life, okay?"

"I'll try."

Natasha vanished into the dark, leaving Liz alone with the castle. As though he knew they had been talking about him, Simon appeared, his face lighting up when he spotted Liz.

"What were you two chatting about?" Simon asked, standing where Natasha had been only moments ago.

"Nothing important," Liz grinned. "We were just clearing up some misunderstandings."

Simon did not push it any further. He stuffed his hands in his pockets, and joined Liz in looking up at the castle. His shoulder brushed against hers, making her forget the cold for a moment.

"I love Scarlet Cove in the autumn," Simon said, casting his finger towards the golden red leaves drifting up the hill. "It's beautiful."

She tore her eyes away from the castle and turned to him. She smiled without realising it, a sudden sense of urgency flooding through her chest. They had missed so much time crossing wires, she suddenly did not want to waste another second. She took a brave step forward as he stared longingly down at her; they were so close she could feel the heat radiating off him.

"Kiss me, Simon," she whispered, her voice silky and low. "Finish what you started."

Instead of the slight hesitance of their almost-kiss at the castle, Simon hooked his finger under Liz's chin, a nervous smile on his lips. He closed his eyes, and their lips finally melted into a kiss.

When they finally parted, they smiled at each other, neither of them wanting to speak; their smiles said it all.

"I guess we should get back," Simon said as he linked his fingers through Liz's. "Everyone will be wondering what's taking us so long."

"Let them wonder," Liz said, grabbing the collar

of Simon's jacket. "I've waited too long for this."

The bitter wind wrapped around them as they kissed outside the Fish and Anchor. It did not matter what had happened, Liz was more certain than ever that everything was going to be just fine.

If you enjoyed *Castle on the Hill*, why not sign up to Agatha Frost and Evelyn Amber's **free** newsletters at **AgathaFrost.com** and **EvelynAmber.com** to hear about brand new releases!

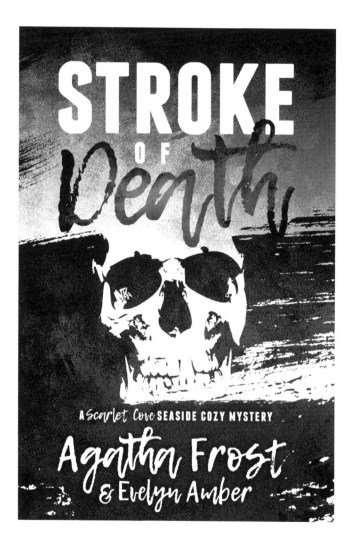

STROKE
OF
Death

A *Scarlet Cove* SEASIDE COZY MYSTERY

Agatha Frost
& Evelyn Amber

Coming soon! Liz and friends are back for another Scarlet Cove case in *Stroke of Death!*

Printed in Poland
by Amazon Fulfillment
Poland Sp. z o.o., Wrocław